GAME OVER

JAMES PATTERSON is one of the best-known and biggest-selling writers of all time. He is the author of the bestselling series for young readers, Witch & Wizard (nominated for the 2011 Nickelodeon Kids' Choice Awards), Maximum Ride, Daniel X and Middle School. This is as well as writing three of the top detective series around – the Alex Cross, Women's Murder Club and Detective Michael Bennett novels – and many other number one bestsellers including romance novels and stand-alone thrillers. He lives in Florida with his wife and son.

James was inspired by his son, who was a reluctant reader, to write books specifically for young readers. He has also formed a partnership with the National Literacy Trust, an independent, UK-based charity that changes lives through literacy. In 2010, James Patterson was voted Author of the Year at the Children's Choice Book Awards in New York.

GAME OVER

James Patterson
and Ned Rust

Published by Young Arrow in 2012

1 3 5 7 9 10 8 6 4 2

First published in Great Britain in 2011 by
Young Arrow
Random House, 20 Vauxhall Bridge Road,
London SW1V 2SA

www.randomhouse.co.uk

Addresses for companies within The Random House Group Limited can be found at:
www.randomhouse.co.uk/offices.htm

The Random House Group Limited Reg. No. 954009

A CIP catalogue record for this book
is available from the British Library

ISBN 9780099544050

The Random House Group Limited supports The Forest Stewardship
Council (FSC®), the leading international forest certification organisation.
Our books carrying the FSC label are printed on FSC® certified paper. FSC is the
only forest certification scheme endorsed by the leading environmental organisations,
including Greenpeace. Our paper procurement policy can be found at:
www.randomhouse.co.uk/environment

MIX
Paper from
responsible sources
FSC® C016897

Printed and bound by CPI Group (UK) Ltd, Croydon, CR0 4YY

For Ruth, for knowing what's what.

—NR

BOOK ONE
ENDANGERED SPECIES

Chapter 1

HELLO! *Buenos dias! Bonjour! Konnichiwa!* It's me, Daniel, here with the critical life lesson of the day: *There's absolutely, positively, no such thing as too much practice or preparation.* Not when it comes to sports, not when it comes to acing your math test, and definitely not when it comes to issues of mortal combat.

Having just died a horrible bloody death in a dusty urban parking lot, I'd clearly forgotten this lesson.

I mean, if you don't even take the time to learn the commands before you start playing a high-end video game like Crown of Thorns IV — the celebrated first-person battlefield shooter with 140 million copies sold and more than twenty million totally obsessed kids playing online at any given moment — you should at least bring along some butter and jam. Because if you're going to be toast, you might as well make the most of it.

Of course, I could have cheated. After all, I am the Alien Hunter, legendary destroyer of the most evil extraterrestrials on Terra Firma (that's Earth for those of you who are new to this stuff). I'm gifted with the ability to create and manipulate anything I can understand, which definitely would include something as basic as cheat codes. I could have given my character Iron Man–style weapons and armor, or I simply could have put my character in a less dangerous place on the battle map. But, like with any game, if you break the rules, it kind of detracts from the experience.

Plus, I was trying *not* to call attention to myself. I was hanging out at the Game Consortium, Inc., flagship store in the high-rise Shinjuku ward of Tokyo, acting like a normal, human teenage boy, doing things that normal, human teenage boys do when they want to play a video game. That includes drooling, grunting, hooting, and standing in line for more than an hour just to have a shot at the latest GC product offerings, as if I were waiting to get onto the Indiana Jones ride at Disneyland. Which is kind of what this place was like.

It was the most high-tech space I'd ever seen, outfitted wall-to-wall with the most cutting-edge gaming software ever devised. Like something you'd expect to see in a secret underground bunker or in NASA's flight command center. The images on the floor-to-ceiling screens and at the holograph stations were crisper and more vivid than reality itself.

The kids waiting in line for a console were all agog in a freaky trance—sweaty, shaking, pale, wide-eyed—like hard-core drug addicts desperate for a fix. I couldn't blame them. The GC's game offerings were truly revolutionary. They always seemed to have better graphics, greater depth of play, and *way* more addictive hunt and battle scenarios than their competitors in the gaming market did.

How, you might ask? The explanation is actually pretty simple. You see, the GC was run by a couple of very, very clever *aliens:* Number 7 and Number 8 on The List of Alien Outlaws on Terra Firma.

In other words, by not one *but two* of my most devious mortal enemies.

Chapter 2

YOU'RE PROBABLY WONDERING how I know the true identities of the owners of the Game Consortium. Fortunately, they're not the only extraterrestrials with outrageously advanced high-tech devices. Allow me to introduce you to Exhibit A: a transcript* of a transmission I'd managed to intercept between Number 7 and Number 8 on my Intergalactic Frequency Sweeper 3000:

> Male voice: *Hello?*
> Female voice: *It's me. Are we still on schedule?*

---

* This dialogue was translated from Kornish, a dialect most often used by certain clans of deep-space Outer Ones.

Male voice: *Yes, just two more hunts to conduct, and we should be able commence Operation Decimation.*

Female voice: *The Mahlerian, then our special friend?*

Male voice: *Yes, of course.*

Female voice: *What a week this is going to be—three legendary species will fall!*

Male voice: *We're making history, my dear.*

Female voice: *You're not at all worried about our friend?*

Male voice: *In some ways, him least of all. His behavior to date has been quite predictable. He's proved himself to be rather dull and unsophisticated.*

Female voice: *Well, let's hope he stays that way. If we manage to pull this off ahead of schedule, we may earn quite a hefty bonus from headquarters.*

Male voice: *And then we can stop this ridiculous charade. I'm so sick of pretending to be human, I could explode! One more stupid press conference, and I may just pull out a blaster and go alien on their butts!*

Female voice: *Relax, dear. Within the month, we'll have to change their scientific name from Homo sapiens to No-mo sapiens.*

[snorting sounds, then an increasingly loud buzzing sound]

[connection lost]

This little exchange had been keeping me awake since I'd first heard it and was precisely why I had come to Tokyo. That snippet had made it clear that Number 7 and

Number 8 were possibly about to wipe the human species off the face of the earth. And on a personal note, I was pretty sure that yours truly was the "special friend" they mentioned. In other words, they knew all about me, and they weren't exactly shaking in their alien booties.

According to The List computer—the alien-tech laptop that has been my bible since I started this gig—going after an alien in the top-twenty deadlies is basically a crapshoot in terms of whether you're going to live or die. But The List isn't some all-knowing machine. It's just an encyclopedia of what we alien hunters and our friends upload into it. Kind of like an ultrasecret wiki about superpowered psychopathic aliens.

All The List had to offer about Number 7 and Number 8 was that the pair had spent the past few years masquerading as Earth's ultimate power couple. In human disguise, they were known as Colin and Ellie Gygax, founders and owners of the Game Consortium, the biggest and most clandestine video-game corporation in the world.

The rest of the info I had was courtesy of Google: the video games created by the Game Consortium were so addicting that phrases like "brainwashing" and "mind control" were sometimes used by concerned parents and teachers when describing them. There were even stories of kids who acted out some of the scenes in the games and landed themselves in detention—or worse.

But GC hadn't technically broken any laws—yet—so governments had done nothing to stop them. I knew it was time for me to act. Unfortunately, the GC's computer systems had proved impossible to hack from the outside. These guys were about twenty times more tech savvy than I was, so electronic surveillance was not exactly easy.

If I wanted to find out more about this place, I would have to get behind the scenes.

Chapter 3

EVIL ENTERTAINMENT EMPIRE or no, I probably could've kept gaming on the showroom floor all day long. But after I lost my thirteenth virtual bout of Extreme Cage Fighter VI, I decided it was time to start the real hunt.

My first move was to head to the back of the store and down a set of stairs to a service corridor, scouting out a way to the Gygax inner sanctum. I guess luck was on my side, because it took me less than five seconds to collide with a poorly disguised alien store clerk who was swinging around the corner with a cart stacked high with boxes.

A sure sign that top-ten List aliens are in the proximity is the presence of low-level hench aliens. In this case, the oddly matched skin around the clerk's eyes and ears, not to mention his orange toupee, were my first clues as to whom I was dealing with.

I immediately materialized a banana peel under one of the cart's wheels, which skidded sideways, causing the cart to tip over — right on me.

"Ahhh!" I yelled, falling to the floor in mock agony. (Well, not exactly "mock." Those boxes were *heavy*.)

"Thisss isss for employeesss only," he hissed in annoyance, accidentally revealing a forked purple tongue. The thing was so long, he could barely keep it in. Clearly, he'd forgotten the mouth part of his human costume that morning.

"I was looking for the restroom," I said, gritting my teeth. He looked me up and down like he had X-ray eyes. "Could you please get these boxes off me?" I continued. "I'm a paying customer, you know."

"You're not welcome in thisss place," he said, his voice dripping with menace. "Go back to Kanssssasss."

I felt the blood drain from my face. Kansas is where my parents raised me from just about infancy until I was three. And Kansas is where my parents were killed — slaughtered in cold blood by The Prayer, Number 1 on The List of Alien Outlaws. Did the clerk know? Had my cover been blown? Were Number 7 and Number 8 watching me? Did they know I was there?

I refused to let paranoia get the best of me and so switched gears.

"I'm sorry to trouble you, sir," I said, extracting myself

from the pile. "I'll be on my way, but let me help you with these boxes first."

The clerk looked momentarily confused, clearly not the cleverest creature to ever step off a UFO. A good tip to remember: politeness and civility throw a goon every time.

I heaved a box that had partially split open. Something metal was poking out, and I shifted the box so I could peer inside.

"No!" The clerk suddenly sounded more anxious than hostile. "I've got it. Pleassse, go back upstairsss. Thisss isss a ssservice corridor only."

"Sorry!" I said with forced cheer. "Have a good day, sssir!"

I was feeling a lot less cheerful than I sounded. What I'd seen inside that box was something no video-game store should need: guns—dozens of them.

And they were definitely not garden-variety man-made handguns that I could easily change into something else. In fact, their Andromedan trinitanium alloy suggested they were imported from a galaxy far, far away—specifically for the purpose of eliminating hard-to-eliminate beings from other planets.

And I just happened to be one of those beings.

I pretended to walk back the way I'd come, then when the clerk wasn't looking I quickly turned myself into a replica of one of the many light fixtures on the walls. The hench alien hastily got his boxes back in order and rushed the cart farther down the hall, where he swiped his ID card at a door bearing a sign that read 従業員.

I hoped to heck that meant "Employees Only" and not "Alien Hunter Execution Chamber."

Chapter 4

I HADN'T YET downloaded all the Japanese language characters to my brain, but at least I'd been studying radio frequency security-lock protocols. By adjusting my eyes down to the RF spectrum and intercepting the ID reader's brief interaction with the clerk's pass, I was able to figure out and memorize his security code.

The next step in my plan would require help, which meant it was time to morph back to human form and summon my best friends Willy, Dana, Joe, and Emma.

Brief interjection here: when I say "summon," I don't mean the way a rich guy might summon his servants. I mean that my best friends are now 100 percent *pure products of my imagination*. It's not like I spend time talking to empty space or cracking up at things that only I can hear. When Joe, Emma, Willy, and Dana are around, everyone can see them, hear them, even shake hands with them if they want to. They're absolutely real. And they're manu-factured by the power of *my mind*.

You might have difficulty understanding what I'm talk-ing about — the power to create and manipulate the atomic structure of things around me is completely "alien" to you earthlings, but it's just part of who I am. It's one of the gifts an alien hunter gets early on and uses pretty frequently. In fact, it's the same power I used to turn myself into that light fixture when the clerk wasn't looking. I also use it to re-create my family, specifically my mom, dad, and sister. Because otherwise I'd be totally alone.

And being alone wasn't an option, at least not then.

"Is this a recon op?" asked Willy, the natural born leader of my gang.

"Yes," I replied, passing them Bluetooth earpieces and phones so we could communicate. "You and Dana, come with me. Joe, you watch this door and give the signal if anybody comes through. Emma, you go up to the main floor and keep an eye on things. If you spot anything that looks like a trap, we want to know about it."

"Aye, aye, Cap'n!" Joe saluted.

I released the lock with a micro-RF broadcast from the palm of my hand. "Let's go."

Willy, Dana, and I hustled down a hall where we found three doors, a small, narrow window in each. We spread out and each peered through one. Mine was dark.

"Over here," Willy whispered, a dim, bluish glow visi-ble through the glass. "One...two...three!"

Defenses ready, we swept into a space that appeared to be a projection booth of some kind.

We were looking down into a theater. Rows and rows of teenagers wearing headphones and holding video-game controllers sat transfixed, eyes glued to monitors built into the backs of the seats in front of them. A stage at the front was filled with riot police and soldiers, and—

Wait a minute! The figures onstage weren't moving. They were just mannequins. But from here, they looked as lifelike as any you'd find at Madame Tussauds wax museum.

Even weirder: intermingled with the police was an assortment of what I'd technically define as thugs, monsters, and all-around bad guys. It looked like the GC might've hired the best special-effects team in Hollywood to put this production together. It was an eerie scene, and it was about to get even eerier.

I looked closer and now could see that a black bag rested near each player's feet. I zoomed in my alien-enhanced vision on one of the screens. They were all playing what appeared to be Crown of Thorns IV, doing battle with video game–sized versions of the thugs onstage.

"Maybe they're beta testing Crown of Thorns V," I speculated. I was pretty certain I'd never seen the levels they were playing, and the graphics were even better than what I'd seen out on the showroom floor.

"Maybe," said Dana, "but what's the deal with the creepy mannequins onstage?"

"Haven't figured out that part yet," I confessed.

It all became clear in a moment when every game display in the theater flickered. Now the players were fighting an on-screen police officer or soldier. Then, after a few minutes, a bright red icon flashed:

CHANGE WEAPONS   CHANGE WEAPONS   CHANGE WEAPONS

In almost perfect synchrony, the kids took weapons from the black bags at their feet. Then, we all held our breath as we watched the armed teenagers charge boldly down the aisles to the stage.

"What the—?" Willy began, as Dana let out a startled cry. But the sounds of gunfire below drowned out any possibility that she'd blown our cover.

In seconds, the good guys had been reduced to smoking, stinking puddles of melted plastic and wire. But if that weren't disturbing enough, I noticed something else: the monsters onstage had been left completely untouched.

The players looked around, almost as if they were in a daze, and a few even slumped to the floor. But some of the more alert ones started circling one another, and I could tell we were seconds away from an all-out brawl.

"I don't think those were regular guns," Willy commented.

"Whatever," said Dana, shaking her head. "That is just *sick*."

"It's even sicker than you think," I agreed, as I ran some

quick math. There were hundreds of millions of GC games and consoles in the world. If the company was able to just flick a switch and turn every player into an armed killer...

"Let's get out of here," I said, just as the screens flashed another message:

GAME OVER   GAME OVER   GAME OVER

The brainwashed players collapsed to the floor.

Chapter 5

AS THE FIVE of us casually strolled out the front door of the Game Consortium—acting like we hadn't just witnessed a dress rehearsal for a massacre—I turned around and looked up at the hulking, looming, skyscraping GC Tower. I couldn't help imagining the eyes of the demonic duo and their subhenchmen following my every move.

"I gotta admit, those games *were* amazing," Willy was saying. "It was like I was playing inside a dream. The way you controlled your avatar almost just by thinking—"

"My personal theory," interrupted Joe, "is that they're using the games to destroy society by making people so hungry they can't think straight. I mean, is it me, or are you guys about to pass out from malnutrition? Quick, let's get some tempura!"

I raised an eyebrow at him. No level of danger or

seriousness ever stops Joe from obsessing about food. The boy must have a forty-gallon stomach.

"I want miso," Emma chimed in. Even she, our most seriously peace-freaky friend, had gotten scarily sucked into the GC's first-person shooter games.

"Guys," I told Joe and Emma soberly. "You didn't see what the rest of us saw in that room. We've got two aliens a couple of steps away from wiping out the entire human species by means of a sinister plot to turn video-game players of the world into nonvirtual killing machines."

Dana's face was still ashen. "He's serious, you two. It was bad. Let me tell you."

"First things first," I said. "It's getting dark, and we have to go find ourselves a secure place to spend the night. Then we'll grab some grub and get these two caught up."

I walked over to a nearby glass-and-chrome bus shelter and scanned the route map. The GC building is located in the Nishi-Shinjuku district of Tokyo. It's a gleaming, bustling, ultradense corporate neighborhood with fancy retail and restaurants around the edges. We needed someplace a little quieter, a little less crowded, a little less likely to be frequented by Number 7 and Number 8's minions.

"Keihin," I said, spotting a sprawling, industrial-looking area on the map down along Tokyo Harbor. It seemed like the kind of place that would have plenty of good spots to hide, and not too many people — or aliens.

"Get on," I said, quickly materializing Pasmo fare cards and handing them out as a bus pulled up. "We've got a bit of a ride ahead of us."

"If I lose my mind from hunger," said Joe, "I'm blaming you."

"You lost your mind a long time ago," Dana quipped.

"I hope it's a scenic route," said Emma. "Apart from Number 7 and Number 8 being here, I'm loving what I've seen of this country so far. It's so . . . *foreign*."

I knew just what she meant, I thought, settling down by a window near the back of the mostly empty bus. Although, technically speaking, *everything* is foreign to me. I am, after all, quite possibly the universe's most displaced orphan. I clutched my arm to my chest as a wave of homesickness washed over me. I call it homesickness; yet I barely have any memory of what my home was like.

I turned and looked behind us out the bus window, hoping to hide my stupid emotions from my friends. The sinister GC Tower still loomed above us, and I again wondered if Number 7 and Number 8 were in there. Probably, I figured. The only things that have been constants in my life are the monsters I'm fated to kill—or die trying.

That and *feeling sorry for myself,* apparently. I needed to get a grip. What was that lesson I had I learned in my last martial arts training session? Something about how if your emotions are getting in the way, you need to tie them to what's going on around you. You need to link them to something practical and immediate.

Like the problem of six aliens masquerading as tattooed young thugs who got on the bus at the next stop.

Chapter 6

IT MUST HAVE been Bad Human Disguise Day here in Tokyo, because those dirtbags wouldn't even have passed for human in a Halloween parade for blind space rangers.

Never mind forked tongues. These guys apparently didn't know that human knees bend *forward*, not *backward*— and that most folks don't have long, hairy tails. Most of them had tucked their tails up their shirts, but the biggest one left his hanging out the top of his leather pants. They clambered aboard like so many overgrown insect-Labrador hybrids and gathered around a tired-looking family of four seated at the front of the bus.

I turned up my hearing (it's a shame you earthlings can't do that), so I could listen in on what they were saying. They were joking among themselves in a horrible attempt at Japanese.

"Nice haul tonight," said one of the shorter ones.

"Not bad," said the tallest and strongest looking of the thugs, the one with the tail hanging out. He also seemed to be the one with the most tattoos—dragons and shogun swords were all up and down his arms and neck. I suddenly realized what they were going for with their gangster exercise clothes and slicked-back hair: they were pretending to be Yakuza, the ruthless Japanese version of America's mafia.

"But remember, we're not just supposed to be collecting revenue; we're supposed to be *acquiring targets for the next hunt*."

"You mean like *these* guys?" said the one wearing the gold-brimmed New York Yankees cap, elbowing the father of the unfortunate family next to him.

The big one leaned over and snuffled at the side of the father's head as the rest of the family sank into their seats in terror.

"Ah, what luck!" he shouted, suddenly wide-eyed and excited. "These are the ones that got away!"

The five of us watched in shock as one of the aliens proceeded to knock out the bus driver with a blow to the back of the head, while another removed what looked like a high-tech staple gun and fired it into the father's shoulder. The poor man screamed in pain and fell to the floor.

I didn't need to say a word to Dana, Emma, Willy, and Joe—we all stormed to the front of the rapidly decelerating bus.

The man wasn't dead—he wasn't even bleeding—but whatever they had just done to him sure didn't tickle.

"All right, tough guys," said Willy, standing up to his full five foot two inches and throwing out his not-exactly-intimidating chest. "Get off this bus, or I'm going to pour a fifty-five-gallon drum of hurt all over your heads."

The big goon turned and for a moment looked at Willy like he'd lost his mind. Then he joined his friends in raucous laughter.

"Maybe we can paralyze them with humor?" suggested Joe as the thugs jumped up on the seats around us and simultaneously drew out the biggest Ginsu knives I'd ever seen.

I leaped ahead of my friends.

"Drop. The. Knives," I said in a voice that, for a second or two, actually made them stop grinning like jackals.

"Kill them," the leader commanded.

"But the boss said no taking humans yet."

"These aren't humans," he replied. "They're gnats."

"They're what?" asked his thickheaded henchman, apparently not knowing what a gnat was and taking him at his word.

"Just *get* them!" ordered the boss.

They sprang toward us, knives flashing. But they didn't realize who they were dealing with. While they were arguing about bugs, I had already decided exactly how I wanted to handle these guys. Having recently played one of the GC's rated-M-for-mature games, Extreme Cage Fighter VI, I morphed myself into one of the most legendary thugs in all video-game lore—Vito the Home Wrecker. Have I mentioned my ability to transform myself into any person or creature that my mind can adequately visualize?

My arms and legs grew long, muscles I didn't normally have rippled all over my body, my neck became massive, my jaw as square as a cinder block, and the next thing I knew I was nearly seven feet tall and over two hundred pounds. The alien thugs instantly recognized me—and my weapon of choice, an oversized baseball bat wrapped in razor wire.

"*Vito?!*" asked one of them, standing stock-still with the rest of his friends.

"Get off this bus," I growled, smashing my club against the floor and causing the bus to rock like we'd just driven over a land mine. "And go tell your superiors that the *Alien Hunter* is here."

"Only if I got your severed head in my hands to prove it!" one of the more dimwitted henchmen yelled. He sprang for me, but I was too quick. The bat smashed into him in midair, and he dropped like a stone.

"Who's next?" I roared. "I've been dying for some batting practice."

The jaws of their pathetic human-costume faces all fell open as I flexed my biceps, covered—as was most of my body—in tattoo portraits of Roman Catholic saints.

"GET OFF!!!" I yelled, and, even before I could cock my club for a second swing, they were clambering over each other to exit the narrow bus door, tails tucked firmly between their legs.

Chapter 7

"CHECK THE DRIVER, Em," I said, assuming my regular form. Emma's got the best medical training of any of us. A few days ago I'd downloaded the entire medical school curricula from Johns Hopkins and Vanderbilt Universities into her consciousness.

Meantime, the rest of us checked on the family. I helped the weary-looking father to his feet and instantly recognized something about him, something about his touch, his energy.

"Wait a second," I said. "You're—"

"Alpar Nokian," he said back to me. "All four of us are. Just like you." In an interesting twist of fate, Alpar Nokians like me are physically identical to you human folks.

"What on earth?"

"Precisely. We were abducted by Number 7 and Number 8's minions two months ago and brought here."

"But why?"

"Best I can figure is we were supposed to be target prac-tice. A training exercise before they went after *you*."

"You know who I am?"

"Didn't you just tell us? You're the Alien Hunter," he said, bowing respectfully.

I had just announced that to the entire bus, hadn't I? My friends had been nagging me to get more rest — it felt like it had been a month since I'd had a full night's sleep — and maybe it was time I started listening to them. I was losing track of what I'd said only minutes ago.

"But if you were captured by Number 7 and Number 8, then why are you on this bus, and why did those fake Yakuza just *re*find you?"

"We were held in isolation for weeks, but then one day our cell door was just, well, it was open. Somebody must have let us out for some reason."

He shrugged and helped his wife and then his kids to their feet. "As to how they found us again just now, I have no idea. Maybe bad luck?"

I nodded. I was getting pretty familiar with what bad luck looked like.

"Thank you for saving us, but we should get going," he said.

"Where will you go?" asked Dana.

"We don't know, but we'll rely on alien ingenuity, yes? We just need to keep moving."

"That's fine, except for one thing," I said, and turned and yelled to Emma. "How's the driver?"

"He'll be fine. Going to have a nice goose egg on the back of his head, but he'll be okay."

"Good. Come here and take a look at this man's shoulder. Those thugs were talking about 'acquiring targets,' right? And something about a hunt? Something makes me think they may have put a transponder in this man, and that we should take it out so they can be on their way without getting tracked down in, like, the next ten minutes."

Emma came back to us, asked the man to remove his button-down shirt, and examined his shoulder.

"I see where it must have gone in, but it's a tiny wound. Maybe a microfiber transmitter?"

"Can we get it out of him?"

"Sure. Why don't you just dematerialize it, Daniel?"

"Well, because I need to know what it is in order to do that. It's not like wishing it away, you know." That was true. I have to know exactly what it is I'm dealing with—and where it is—or it could be, um, a little dangerous. I mean, I didn't want to put an unnecessary hole in the man, or sever an artery.

"I trust you," said the man.

"I'm an alien hunter, not a surgeon, sir."

"You're the Alien Hunter—you can do *anything*."

"Don't believe the hype," I replied. "My so-called powers only work when I have enough time to think something through, and when I truly *understand* what it is I'm trying to do."

Seriously—it's not as easy as you might think.

28

Chapter 8

"WE'RE GOING TO need a portable ultrasound scanning unit," Emma said. "Try the Yokohiro Medical Institute servers."

"On it," I replied, whipping The List laptop out of my backpack and conducting a quick search. Y-O-K-O-H-I— there it was. And there was the ISP of their internal server stacks. And then it was just a few more steps before, voilà; there were the manufacturer's design specs. And now that I knew what it was and could see exactly how it worked—

"Perfect," said Emma, looking over the newly material-ized device in her hands. It basically resembled a police radar gun. She aimed it at the man's shoulder and had me look into the viewfinder. A glowing mass, about two inches long, spiraled through the flesh of his shoulder, perilously close to the axillary nerve. I let my brain absorb the image—the dimensions, the orientation—and was overcome with a new appreciation for what it is surgeons do.

And then, just like that, because I could *see* it, I teleported the transmitter out of the man's shoulder and into the palm of my hand.

It looked like a curly silver wire. I zoomed in my eyes and did a quick study of its circuitry and transmission patterns. If this was a device Number 7 and Number 8 were routinely using, it would be useful to know something about it. Then I materialized a glass beaker of nitric acid and dropped it in—a pretty quick way to destroy the thing for good.

"Can you please give me the names you've been using here?" I asked.

"We are the Murkamis," replied the father. "I am Eigi. This is my wife, Etsuyo; my daughter, Miyu; and my son, Kenshin."

I introduced myself and my friends, but the real reason I needed their names was for a set of documents I produced right on the spot: Japanese passports, credit cards, and airline tickets to London—a place I knew to be recently free of alien infestations (read Book Three if you're curious) and where they should be safe for a while.

"Take these and get your family out of the country," I said. "Things are about to get pretty hot here in Tokyo."

"I couldn't possibly take—"

"He made them out of thin air," Willy said. "It's not like you're *taking* anything from him. Trust me."

The man thought a moment, then nodded. Then we all

hugged. What can I say? We Alpar Nokians are big into public displays of affection.

"Hurry," said Dana. "You may have destroyed it, but that transmitter was working for a few minutes there. Other killers may be on the way, even as we speak."

Chapter 9

NUMBER 7 AND NUMBER 8, Colin and Ellie Gygax to the rest of the world, were having a romantic candlelit dinner in the penthouse apartment of the Game Consortium Tower. They were sitting at a priceless room-length table milled from the dense, richly veined wood of an extinct species of alien tree. And set in the middle of the table in front of them was a lacquered bowl made from the shell of an extinct tortoise-like alien.

"Ah," said Number 7, slurping away at the soup it contained. "Endangered species jambalaya always takes my mind off my troubles."

"Do you like it?"

"You've out*done* yourself, my dear. Say, is that the Nicolarian I detect? The fruity, almost cherry-like overtones?"

"Very good, honey," said Number 8. "It certainly is."

One of several meats in the soup came from a Nicolarian, a species that resembled a gray-haired boa constrictor. Employees of Number 7 and Number 8 had just hunted the only one left last week, and now the two of them were *eating* it.

"Oh, *Colin*," Number 8 went on, giggling. It was so very droll to call each other by their fake human names.

"Ah," said Number 7, chuckling along. "Perhaps there *is* some part of this unbearable charade I'll miss."

"I don't think so; we won't have time to miss anything." Number 8 laughed.

"Once we launch the 5G editions and the gamers start tearing this world apart—"

"And once we have personally wiped out the last Alpar Nokian—"

"Ah, yes. Play the video feed. Let's see him one more time!"

Suddenly, the floor-to-ceiling windows overlooking Tokyo went opaque and lit up with a high-resolution picture of a teenage boy climbing down off a bus with a homeless family.

"Will you just look at him?" Number 7 said. "So young, so firm, so vital, so—"

"Absolutely *delectable*," said Number 8, drooling into their shared bowl of soup.

"And soon to be the very last of his kind," said Number 7.

"As these annoying humans would have to admit about their caviar and truffles: *scarcity* is the very best seasoning."

"Well said, *Colin*," Number 8 replied. "Let's savor this one *together*, shall we?"

"Absolutely, Ellie," said Number 7. And then, somehow, the two of them morphed into a shimmering cloud of gray specks that hovered over the bowl and consumed every last particle of soup.

And then they—or it—descended on the kitchen to eat the scraps.

Chapter 10

IF I HAD realized that the Gygaxes had been watching me on a giant video screen as they ate the last of some poor endangered (now extinct) species, I might have been a little more thorough about checking my surroundings for the equipment they must have been using to track me. But I was a little busy at the moment, squaring off with a rather unlikely opponent.

"You can't lose touch with your *key* like that," said the little girl, Miyu, Eigi Murkami's daughter.

The little she-devil had just delivered a sharp blow to my solar plexus, knocking all the air out of me and making my vision go gray.

"Actually," I said, wincing as I got back up off the dojo's bamboo floor, "I don't have a key or even a wallet, for that matter."

"Not k-e-y; *ki!*" she barked at me.

"Ah," I said. "You mean it's another word. Can you please give me the language of origin? And use it in a sentence?"

I guess she hadn't seen any National Spelling Bees lately because she gave me a look like I'd lost my mind. I had been hoping to distract her with a laugh, but this would have to do. As she grimaced, I lunged forward and locked her in a jujutsu embrace, setting her up for a devastating fulcrum throw.

But she was having none of it. She countered with a piece of *kansetsu waza*—joint-locking technique—a leg swipe that made my left knee buckle, and the next thing I knew I was looking up at her from the floor.

"In English, you would spell it k-i. *Ki,*" she said. "It sort of means energy. Now, do you submit?" she asked, driving her heel into my windpipe even harder than before.

"Restraint, Miyu," urged her mother, turning to us as she waited for Dana to get back to her feet. Dana seemed to have had about as much luck sparring with Eigi's wife, Estuyo, as I had been having with their daughter. And Joe, Willy, and Emma also seemed to be spending an inordinate amount of time on the bamboo floor—sparring, as they had been, with Eigi and his son, Kenshin.

Both for company and because generally there is safety in numbers, we had invited my fellow Alpar Nokians to spend the night with us before they headed off to Narita Airport in the morning.

The smart thing to do would have been to get some

sleep—I had some aliens to hunt, and the Murkamis had a long flight ahead of them—but I guess I was just excited about having people from my home planet around. And what with us happening upon an abandoned martial arts studio, it seemed only natural that we would start talking about the martial arts. I've had quite a bit of training over the years, and the Murkamis professed to be slightly expert themselves—black belts, in fact, just like me. So, from there, it was only natural that all nine of us would end up on the dojo floor in a friendly little tournament. Right?

The only problem was that even though I had thought I'd be the one giving pointers, the clinic was clearly shaping up to be *for*, not *by*, me.

"Tell me," I said, rubbing my neck and getting back up as Miyu resumed a defensive crouch. "Exactly what part of Alpar Nok are you guys from?"

"We learned these martial arts here on Earth," said Eigi, helping Joe and Willy back to their unsteady feet. "Just as you did."

Well, that much I believed. If people on Alpar Nok had known how to fight like this, there'd be a lot more of us alive right now. Seriously, these guys knew every move in the book, and a bunch I'd never heard of. I guessed maybe that was the advantage of getting your training in Japan instead of from your imaginary father in America, as I had.

I untied the black belt from my waist and offered it to Miyu. Some may say I'm stubborn to a fault, but, believe me, I know when I'm outclassed.

"Honorable Alien Hunter," said Eigi, coming over to

me. "There is no need to turn in your belt. You are a worthy opponent for any black belt of the second or third degree."

"So, you guys are like seventh degree or something?"

"Miyu is *forty*-seventh, but she is still young. The rest of us, as you might expect, are higher degrees than that. Would you like some training?"

I shrugged and looked over at my exhausted, demoralized friends. They were nodding their heads as vigorously as they could through the pain. I guessed it wouldn't hurt us any to pick up some tips.

Chapter 11

WE CONTINUED THE training until my friends and I were so sore we couldn't move. I made Emma, Willy, and Joe disappear, with the excuse that they needed to recover, but Dana seemed to want to stick around for a while. Which was just fine with me.

"You were so good, Daniel," Dana said.

"What do you mean? At sparring?" Dana's one of the sincerest people I know, but I briefly wondered if she was making fun of me.

"For not beating them," she said.

"But they kicked my butt," I said. "Even little Miyu."

"But that was just because you played by the rules. You could have easily used your powers to beat them."

"Assuming I'd had even a second to think straight,

maybe you're right. But that wasn't the point. They're friends, they're from Alpar Nok—they're good guys."

"I'm just saying...you were very disciplined and mature. I'm impressed is all."

"Aren't I always disciplined and mature?"

"You mean like taking us halfway around the world to go after Number 7 and Number 8 with no plan and next to no preparation? Um...no."

"Dana, you know as well as I do that they're about to make a move. I had no choice but to step in."

"It doesn't have to be all or nothing, Daniel. You don't need to put yourself in harm's way every single time. You've been very lucky but—"

I was about to tell her she sounded like my mother, but it occurred to me that she might take it the wrong way. And, anyhow, I was feeling homesick enough without bringing my mother into the picture.

Dana and I looked over at the Murkamis. They were getting ready for bed, and Etsuyo was reading a bedtime story to the two kids—a chapter of the Japanese translation of *The Great Gilly Hopkins*.

"You know," said Dana, "sometimes I forget that if we were on Alpar Nok, we'd still be living at home with our parents."

"On Alpar Nok—" I stopped, deciding not to remind her where she'd really be if she were still there...*dead*. Victim of one of the worst extraterrestrial invaders in the universe. "If we were back home, we might have been packed up in a crate like this family," I said. "That's why I'm here on Earth. That's why we're in Tokyo right now."

Dana looked at me, and I saw something in her eyes, an emotion I'm not sure I know what to call, but I knew whatever was going on behind her brilliant blues was intense. Maybe even as intense as the feeling in my chest right then. Why was my heart beating the way it was beating? Why did I feel apprehensive and excited and like I just wanted to keep talking with her all night and maybe we could even go for a walk and—

Dana smiled inscrutably and said good night, pulling her sleeping bag up over her head.

"Good night, Dana," I said and rolled over and sighed. I might be responsible for her existence, but clearly I had little or no control over what she did.

I refluffed my pillow for the eightieth time and wondered if I would ever fall asleep. Confusion about girls isn't exactly the most relaxing thing in the world, is it?

Chapter 12

ON THE GROUNDS of a shrine in a residential area of Ota, a district on the south side of Tokyo, a sleek black cat rested atop a high garden wall and cried softy, its blue-white eyes shining up into the starry night.

There was a certain peacefulness about the spot, a tranquility that almost gave the cat a sense of hope after the past several hours of panicked chaos. Somebody or—more accurately, several somebodies—had been *hunting* it all night long.

And it wasn't over yet. A gunshot ripped through the darkness, and the cat sprang from its perch.

It was a tremendous leap. From the force of its legs alone, the cat had landed a good twenty feet from the wall. And then, as it cleared the bushes that ran parallel, it *sprouted wings* that glinted and gleamed like peacock feathers in the moonlight.

The cat banked steeply, clearing the garden gate and hurtling down the alleyway, a look of steely resolution—a resolution to *live*—in its now glowing, slit-pupiled eyes.

It would not be an easy resolution to keep. As the bullet ricocheted above the just-blossoming cherry trees, the hunter bounded over the wall, its grasshopper-style rear legs disloding enormous divots of soil from the ground.

And now the hunter, too, opened its wings—leathery and ridged with a network of scarlet veins—and banked out over the alley. It howled like a banshee as it flew through the night air, a gale of dust blowing up off the ground.

The cat's pursuer was not just bigger, stronger, and faster; it was also high-tech. A pair of wraparound goggles tracked the quarry's flitting figure and illumined it like a torch in a dark field. It also had a gun in each of its three forehands.

The cat's reflexes were already dull from exhaustion. Every time it had shaken its pursuer, another one somehow found it again. Still, it hadn't been transported halfway across the galaxy—the last of its kind—because it was prone to giving up.

The hunter was gaining—maybe just ten yards behind now. The cat's eyes suddenly shone like high beams, and, right then, from glands in each of its hind legs, it sprayed two clouds of nitric acid into the air.

In an instant, the attacker's lungs convulsed in mortal pain, its organs spilling into one another as the powerful acid destroyed the membranes between them, causing the great insect-like beast to slam into the cobblestones and explode as if it were a water balloon filled with black yogurt.

The bird-cat trilled with satisfaction and shot straight up into the night, clearing the artfully stacked roofs of a pagoda, and then arcing south toward a massive oil refinery on the banks of Tokyo Harbor.

Chapter 13

THE BIRD-CAT DOVE amid the hulking reef of refinery towers, pipes, valves, hoses, tanks, and heat exchangers, searching for a place to hide, a spot to get its light-filled heart back under control.

Mahlerian bird-cats are unique in all of nature for having, deep inside their chests, an organ that basically functions on the principle of nuclear fusion. In other words, with the same intense energy that fires the sun.

It takes place on a more modest scale, of course, and with a few mere atoms at work, rather than the billions of tons of matter that make up a star. And the power source never fails, except when the animal—through illness, stress, injury, or other trauma—loses control of the self-sustaining life force.

You see, when a fusion reaction escalates past containment, there's an explosion—an explosion that, though on a smaller scale, is still of the sort that occurs when you set off a hydrogen bomb. What could happen next was a big reason Mahlerian bird-cats had the intergalactic renown they did.

The bird-cat dove down, deep into the bowels of the refinery, into a dense forest of carbon-cracking tubes safely hidden from any sky- or ground-traveling passersby who might still be searching for it.

Could it have finally given the slip to its pursuers?

Unfortunately, not one, but *seven* other alien safari hunters—card-carrying, paying members of Number 7 and Number 8's exclusive Hunt Club—were tracking the microfiber transponder that had been implanted in the bird-cat's rear leg, and were even now converging on the refinery. And the safari hunters weren't merely concerned with hunting down the bird-cat; they also wanted to beat each other to the kill.

The first two hunters on the scene saw a third streaking ahead of them in an unauthorized skycar. It was a flagrant violation of Hunt Club rules to use nonnative transportation, so they didn't hesitate to atomize both skycar and cheating hunter.

The explosion attracted the attention of the four other hunters, who aimed and fired at the two who had first used their weapons. In a matter of seconds, an all-out alien war was taking place on the grounds of the refinery.

The bird-cat heard the explosion too—and then more weapon fire and shouting—and quickly fled east toward the Pacific Ocean. Perhaps its relentless pursuers would have trouble tracking it to the depths of the Mariana Trench.

But even as it readied itself to bound over the barbed-wire top of the chain-link fence and into the inky harbor beyond, two humanoid figures leaning against the hood of a limousine simultaneously fired high-intensity micro-wave ray guns.

Because microwaves travel at the speed of light, there was no escape this time. The rays converged, instantly incinerating the bird-cat, and thereby releasing all the raw galvanic energy the creature contained. A blue-white blast about thirty yards in diameter seared the eyes of anybody foolish enough to have been looking that way. A split second later, the entire refinery exploded in a mushroom cloud of superheated petrochemicals.

"That was unfortunate," said Number 7 to Number 8, referring more to the loss of the priceless quarry than to the incineration of a handful of their high-paying club members. There were always more clients.

"But it had to be done," replied Number 8 as they stashed their microwave ray guns in the trunk of the limo. "We can't leave evidence around for the humans—or our Alien Hunter friend—just now."

"So true, my dear," said Number 7, getting behind the wheel and driving the limousine back toward Tokyo. "Surprise, after all, is the most crucial element in our plan."

"Still, Colin," said Number 8, "one can't help but be saddened at being denied the chance to sample Mahlerian bird-cat kebabs."

"I hear they don't need much *hot* sauce, Ellie," he replied, and they both broke out laughing.

Chapter 14

THE SHOCK WAVE from the exploding refinery rattled windows across Tokyo, and all of us in the dojo sat bolt upright in our sleeping bags.

"What was *that!?*" asked Emma, voicing the question in all of our sleep-addled heads.

"I believe," said Eigi, his mind spinning with the quick and precise analysis that only an alien could have, "that the Game Consortium's Hunt Club just managed to kill a Mahlerian bird-cat."

"A Mahlerian *bird-cat?*" I yelled in surprise. "I thought they were extinct!"

"*Now* they are," replied Etsuyo.

"The last specimen was being held in an intergalactic preserve for cloning purposes, but Number 7 and Number 8 stole it and brought it here. We saw it while we were being held captive."

"He was my friend," said Kenshin, choked up.

"Why would they bring it all the way to Earth just to kill it?" I asked.

"It's all part of one of their video games—only, of course, they're more than video games," explained Eigi. "Number 7 and Number 8 didn't just get into this line of work here on Earth. They've been at it for millennia, on many other planets, with many other races. And the final stage of their efforts is always *extinction*. They take great pride in being the ones to destroy the last vestiges of a species. This Hunt Club of theirs is actually a safari game they run for the best—that is, winning—players of past conquests. It's something they do to test out their systems when they arrive at a new planet. And it also helps them tie up any loose ends from the planets they've left."

"Their virtual hunting games have become real hunting games?" I asked.

Eigi nodded.

"But how?"

"Essentially, they've gotten their players so addicted that their habits force them to cross over into the real world," continued Eigi.

"Like what we saw in that creepy theater," Dana said quietly.

"In fact, these 'winners' are actually still willingly paying them for the experience," Eigi went on. "They're here to track quarry through the streets of Tokyo and all over

Japan. That is, in fact, why *we* were brought here. We're among the last of the Alpar Nokians—we're close to extinction, too—so we qualify as prey. And so, of course, do you."

"That's *sick!*" bawled Emma, our official Animal Planet addict. "Why would they *do* that!?"

"Who can know the heart of the beast?" asked Eigi.

"A veterinary heart surgeon?" asked Joe, eliciting not a single laugh. This was *not* a funny situation.

Clearly, I needed to put a stop to this and take out Number 7 and Number 8. Both of them at once. Both of them, even though I hadn't even managed to lay eyes on them yet, except in their human forms on television and on the Internet.

As if reading my mind—which maybe she can because, after all, she came out of it—Dana said, "Maybe we should back off and find some other way, Daniel."

I ignored her. "Eigi, do you know where Number 7 and Number 8 live? Are they in the GC Tower?"

"Yes, I think they're up on the top floor most of the time. We sometimes heard our guards saying things about going up to the penthouse, so I assume that's where they stay."

"You're *not* going up there, Daniel," said Dana.

"Well, not there, precisely," I said to her with a wink.

Chapter 15

THE SQUEEGEE IN my hand was shaking so much that every window I tried to clean ended up looking like a chalk-covered snake had slithered across it. The reason for my nerves was that I was standing in a window-washing gondola six hundred and sixty-three feet above the street. I was attempting to pose as a window washer, but I don't think I was exuding the necessary degree of confidence or indifference to heights. The street below me — at least the one time I stupidly looked down — was spinning like I was in one of those tilt-a-hurl rides at the state fair. And the way the wind was buffeting and rocking the narrow, low-railed platform...let's just say I was seriously regretting that third helping of tempura Joe had convinced me to eat.

Coming up here had seemed like a good idea when I'd been safely down on the ground. The Mode Gakuen Cocoon

Tower—among the coolest skyscrapers on earth—is a fifty-story teardrop-shaped structure encased in a lattice-work of curving dark glass and white aluminum. And it happens to be located just across the street from the GC Tower, where Number 7 and Number 8 keep both their official business and their residence.

Unfortunately, the Mode Gakuen's unconventional shape means it doesn't have much in the way of a flat roof on which to sit. When you're trying to spy on two evil penthouse-dwelling aliens across the street, that can be a bit of a problem. Especially when you're not so keen on heights to begin with.

Of course, two hours into my reconnaissance mission, it was all seeming like a big, fat, needlessly-high-up-in-the-air waste of time. Boy, can aliens be boring. The only thing I'd discovered about Number 7 and Number 8 so far was that they were Internet junkies. They hadn't done *any*thing but surf the Web on their laptops. And their surfings weren't exactly the stuff of legend. Other than reading some news stories about the big refinery explosion last night, they mostly seemed to be interested in landmark Tokyo buildings and—get this—parenting websites. Weird. Boring, but weird.

I was just about to call it a night when I suffered the worst bout of vertigo ever. And it had nothing to do with the height or the unsteadiness of the horrible window-cleaning gondola.

Someone had just emerged from the private penthouse elevator and entered their suite. Someone with a striking

53

resemblance to an overgrown mantis with wild dread-locks and the most evil-looking eyes you could imagine.

It was Number 1 — *The Prayer!*

My parents' killer . . . my ultimate nemesis . . . the dark-est stain in all my nightmares.

Chapter 16

I WANTED TO run and hide. I wanted to teleport myself to another continent or, heck, another planet. But this was Number 1. I couldn't afford to be scared. I couldn't afford to get distracted. And, most of all, I couldn't afford to miss this chance to find out what he was doing here.

And that was a problem, because he was a street-width away from me behind a wall of insulated glass. Unless I wanted to get closer and run the risk of being seen, it was going to be hard to find out what they were saying.

Hard, but not impossible…especially for a kid who'd recently downloaded the Massachusetts Institute of Technology's Acoustical Engineering PhD curriculum into his cerebellum. I zoomed in my eyes on the glass of the floor-to-ceiling penthouse windows to the point at which I could see the vibrations caused by my enemies' words.

And from there, it was a simple matter of translating the vibrations back into sounds and...

"That poor, poor kitty cat. What is *wrong* with you two?!" asked Number 1, swiveling his head back and forth in his creepy rendition of a disapproving head shake. His voice carried a note of amusement, but Number 7 and Number 8's obvious nervousness made it clear he wasn't totally joking.

"I have told you before," he said, his eyes flashing (only that's not really the right word because it wasn't light coming out of them—it was *darkness*). "And I'll tell you again— there is only *one* creature I need you to hunt to extinction, and that's Graff and Atrelda's unfortunate leave-behind. Little whatever-his-name-is."

"He calls himself Daniel," replied Number 8, timidly.

"What day of the week is it?" said Number 1, rising up on his hind legs and glowering at her.

"Tuesday."

"Then *I* want *you* to call him *Thursday Night Soup*."

"But what if he time-travels back to Monday?" asked Number 7.

"I've seen to it that he can't do any more of his time-travel tricks," Number 1 said, annoyed. "Now do your job and *hunt him down*."

"Yes, sensei," said Number 7 and Number 8 in unison, bowing and backing away from him.

"And stop acting like humans!" screamed Number 1. "You two are taking this playacting too far. Between your tabloid antics and the way your so-called son's been behaving lately, you'll probably end up going native on me."

"Of course, master," said Number 7 and Number 8, like they shared voice. It was a little creepy how they did that, actually. Maybe it was a talent that came with being married a really long time...

"Listen to me!" Number 1 barked. "I cannot afford *any more* screw-ups. I'm having to spend enough time recruiting and training replacements for Numbers 6, 5, and 3 without worrying about two *more* openings to fill."

"Don't worry, master. We're on schedule."

"I need you to be more than *on* schedule. You need to be *ahead* of schedule," said Number 1, straightening up to his full height and glaring down at the human-looking couple. "We've had an unfortunate setback," he said. "A Pleionid has landed here on Earth."

"A *Pleionid?*" asked Number 7.

I was familiar with the name. Pleionids were a species of legendary genius and unique telepathic abilities. Unfortunately, they were also complete pacifists and had offered next to no resistance when Outer One poachers had invaded their world. Theirs was one of those legendary extinctions, much like the dodo bird or the passenger pigeon here on Earth.

"But they're extinct!!" blurted Number 8.

The impatient look Number 1 gave her was enough to remove any doubt. "I don't care whether you kill it, or him, first—but by no means may you let them make contact with each other...unless it's as ingredients in one of your meals. Do you understand me?"

Number 7 and Number 8's ravenous, drooling expressions

made it clear that there was no mission they'd have more willingly undertaken. For these two hunters of endangered species to receive a shot at one the most legendary of all interstellar creatures—

Number 1 backed in to the open elevator, his insect eyes now glowing red.

"Don't even *think* of failing me."

"Oh, no, master. We won't!" they yelled as the polished stainless steel doors slid closed.

I gripped the railing of the window-cleaning gondola with both hands. My head was spinning. Number 1 here in Tokyo? The monster that had killed my parents and probably orchestrated the near genocide of my race?

Had I really just seen him with my own eyes? Had I really just overheard his plans?

Or was it all a trick? Had Number 7 and Number 8 known I'd be watching? Was it just a red herring to throw me off? Was I really supposed to believe there was a living Pleionid somewhere in this city? And *what* was that part about how Number 1 had seen to it that I could no longer time-travel? I'd never doubted myself this much before. I didn't know what to believe...

But I didn't have any more time to ponder it right then. The elevator doors opened again and disgorged a figure far less intimidating yet in some ways more disturbing than Number 1.

Chapter 17

I'D SEEN A lot of aliens in my day, but until that moment I'd never seen one wearing Adidas.

The boy who'd just entered the apartment of Number 7 and Number 8 looked to be about my age, with jet-black hair and piercing dark eyes, and wearing a tattered wool sweater and blue jeans. There was something deeply sad about him, like somebody close to him had died and he didn't want to talk about it. He looked like a decent kid. Which was bizarre considering this was apparently Number 7 and Number 8's *son*.

"Kildare, my boy," said Number 7, turning away from his computer screen, which right then was filled with engineering schematics of some antennas located on the second-tallest structure in Tokyo, the famed Tokyo Tower. "You'll never guess who was just here."

"The Supernanny," replied Kildare, "come to give you two some parenting pointers."

"What is he talking about, Colin?" asked Number 8.

"As usual, Ellie," said Number 7, "I have no idea." He turned back to his son with a stern expression. "We were just called on by none other than *The Prayer*."

A flicker of surprise crossed Kildare's face, quickly masked by a shrug.

"Do you even know who that is?" Number 8 prodded, disgust creeping into her tone.

The boy had looked ready to fire a sarcastic retort but thought better of it. Instead, he turned and headed toward the kitchen.

"I thought not. He's Number 1, my dear, ignorant child. On *The List*." No response from Kiladare. "And there's something else you should know," continued his mother.

Kildare paused as he reached the kitchen door.

"There's a *Pleionid* here in Tokyo."

The boy spun around, a look approaching panic on his face.

"What!? They're extinct!"

"All but one. One that came here to interfere with our plans."

"But aren't they pacifists?"

"That may be, but we think it's intending to pass on information that our *non*pacifist enemies might use," explained his mother.

"All of that is immaterial," Number 7 jumped in. "The

60

fact is that the hunt for the last Pleionid will be the stuff of legend, a once-in-a-lifetime opportunity for any hunter."

"In fact," said Number 8, "your father and I have been talking, and, since your sixteenth colony cycle is approaching, we think *you* should be *hunt leader* on this one."

"What a glorious first kill it could be for you!" said Number 7. "Much like my own, when I caught and killed the last Reticulated Shandlerite on Guldbrekker 11."

It looked to me like all the blood had drained from Kildare's face. "Sure, Dad. Say, I just remembered..." He hesitated, turning back to the private elevator. "I left some equipment at school. I have to go."

"Kildare! We've already talked about your *forgetting* things all of the time. We are not a family—much less a species—that *forgets* things."

"But I have to go get it or I won't be able to finish my science project."

"And then what?" asked his father. "I know we asked you to blend in and learn their ways; but this interest of yours in school—it's *unseemly,* Kildare."

"I can't blend in if I fail out."

"Well," said Number 8, looking quite human in her motherly disapproval, "make sure you're back in time for dinner. The hunt starts in two days, and you'll need extra rest so you'll be ready."

"Your first hunt! Ah, that'll get you past this school bug!" said Number 7, rubbing his hands together and leaning back in his computer chair.

Kildare grimaced and disappeared into the elevator.

"This will be just the thing to get him back on track," declared Number 7. "There's no way he'll be able to deny his heritage after tasting the thrill of *the hunt*."

"I hope you're right," said Number 8. "Should we put up some fail-safes so he doesn't get hurt?"

"No, let him prove himself. If he doesn't rise to the challenge..."

"Of course, you're right, dear," said Number 8, coming up behind her husband and rubbing his shoulders. "We can always make another."

As Number 7 stood and began returning her affections, I quickly turned off my "hearing" and looked away from their window. Not only am I really *not* into watching aliens smooch, but I didn't have much time to figure out where their son was going. He was definitely up to something.

Fortunately, one thing faster than high-speed elevators is instantaneous teleportation. Of course, you have to know exactly where it is you're teleporting to or you can find yourself lodged in a solid object, with some pretty unpleasant results. But by now, I'd made a thorough study of the GC building's layout and knew exactly where the penthouse elevator stopped. In the blink of an eye, I disguised myself as a security guard and teleported myself to the lobby.

Only problem was, when the elevator doors opened up, Kildare wasn't there.

Chapter 18

I PULLED DOWN the brim of my security cap and stepped into the empty express elevator. There was no sign of Kildare, but the panel made it pretty clear where he'd gone. The lobby and the penthouse each had a button, but there was another button to select. It was labeled with the Japanese character for "service," and, based on its position in the panel, it seemed to be the floor directly below the penthouse. I hit the button.

The elevator rose quickly—so quickly my ears popped—and opened into a space quite different than the one occupied by Number 7 and Number 8. No polished obsidian floors or exotic furnishings here. This was a filthy, fluorescently lit, windowless room filled with all kinds of Dumpsters, washers and dryers, cleaning supplies, and a very tired-looking, stooped old woman in a crisp white cleaning uniform. She immediately put down her mop and bowed at me as I stepped out of the elevator.

"Did you see a kid come through here?" I asked in Japanese.

"No, sir," she replied.

I could tell she was lying. Maybe the kid had threatened her? Maybe his parents had?

Just then, a large chute dropped down from the ceiling, and a load of dirty pots and revolting soup bones rained into the middle of the floor. The old woman picked up her mop.

"You have to clean this entire place yourself?"

"Whenever the masters are home, yes, of course," she said, moving toward the fresh mountain of filth.

My heart went out to her. Getting this place passably clean would have taken a team of professional cleaners a week...or an Alpar Nokian cleaning robot approximately ten minutes.

I quickly materialized one of the compact white machines I'd known from my childhood.

"How did you—?"

"Make a cleaning machine out of thin air?"

She nodded.

"I'm not going to tell you so that you have plausible deniability, okay?"

"What?"

"Somebody comes in here and asks you where that machine came from, and you can honestly say, 'I don't know.' Right?"

"I don't know how to thank you," she said, bowing to me over and over again as the white machine zipped around the room obliterating every piece of trash it encountered.

"Can you please tell me where that kid went? I promise I'm not here to hurt him."

She looked me in the eyes. "Well, if you *promise* not to harm him. . . . Sometimes he goes through *there*."

She was pointing at a metal grate—an air vent—in the wall. Judging by the worn hinges, it had been opened and closed many times.

"He's a nice boy," she said. "Not at all like his parents."

I nodded, popped the cover, and climbed down into the dark metal duct.

When I put my mind to it, I can make my nose more sensitive than a bloodhound's. I'm talking the ability to detect parts per *trillion*. It's a weird sensation, being able to smell things that strongly—and it can cause some serious nausea if you come across a bad odor like, you know, brussels sprouts—but it can be a huge help in cases like this where you're climbing around a skyscraper's branching ductwork in pitch dark.

I followed Kildare's scent, which was definitely not human, to a small room that was clearly his lair. I knew it was his, because I'm pretty well acquainted with the living habits of my race—not of Alpar Nokians but Teenage Boyians.

The small custodian's closet was dominated by a dangerous-looking mountain of clothing, shoes, and Snickers wrappers. To one side, a metal locker plastered with Linkin Park and other rock-band stickers had been turned on its side to support an Xbox 360 console, a flat-screen television, a broken remote control, and a pile of papers and school books.

I picked up one of the books and looked it over. It was a textbook with a close-up of a moth's face on the cover. I managed to translate the Japanese characters to "Zoology: A Complete Survey." "Kildare Gygax" was written inside the cover—both in Japanese characters and our more familiar Roman alphabet. Below that was the name and address of a local secondary school.

As I returned the book to the makeshift desk, I noticed that the overturned locker was completely blocking the only door to the room. Did that mean that Kildare came and left only through the vent?

I understood the need for privacy—especially with parents like his—but it seemed like it would be pretty inconvenient to forever be clambering around in those dark, cramped vents to get in and out of here.

And why were there *two* sleeping bags, not one? And why was one so much smaller than the other?

I quickly examined them. They'd each been slept in, and recently. The bigger one smelled exactly like the trail in the vents and must have been Kildare's. But the little one—it could have been an infant's sleeping bag, and it smelled like nothing I'd ever come across. I mean, I don't even know what to compare it to. It was kind of sweet, but not like perfume and not like candy. It just smelled *good* somehow, if that makes any sense.

But there weren't any other clues, at least that I could find. If the big bag was Kildare's, whose was the little one? A little brother's?

I didn't have any idea what was going on. And what about Number 1? Had he just been checking in on Number 7 and Number 8, or was he here for something else? If he were to join forces with those two, the scales wouldn't just tip the wrong way; they'd fall right off the counter.

A chill ran down my spine, and I spun around, but no one was there.

Strange. Usually when I have the feeling that I'm being watched, I'm right.

Chapter 19

THERE WAS ONLY one reasonable thing to do to ease my nerves: check in to a luxury hotel.

The Fujiya Hotel, a Western-style hotel dating to 1878, is down in Hakone, a mountain resort town south of Tokyo. Charlie Chaplin, Helen Keller, Dwight D. Eisenhower, John Lennon, kings of England, and, of course, emperors of Japan—you name a celebrity or VIP from the past couple centuries, and if they visited Japan, chances are they stayed at the Fujiya.

You reach it by bullet train, not a bad hour-long hop out of Tokyo, and then take a switchback train up into the hot spring–studded mountains. It's inviting and beautiful and classy and just the sort of spot where you can escape from the modern hubbub and luxuriate in true old-world opulence, replete with the most deluxe room service you've ever seen.

I placed my order as soon as I got to the room: "Yes, I'd like eight bowls of the Imperial consommé, two dozen orders of the assorted sashimi, seven gratin-of-shrimp with the sole Queen Elizabeth II, eight Chaliapin steaks—actually, better make that nine—and why don't you throw in twenty orders of shrimp tempura. As for drinks, I'd like two pitchers of fresh-squeezed orange juice, four liters of Coke, two liters of Sprite, three liters of Pineapple Crush, and some of that fancy sparkling water—what's it called—Pellegrino? Oh, and dessert. Do you have baked Alaska? Great, how many people does it serve? Yes, in that case, I'd like three of those too. *Domo arigato.*"

And then—so you don't think I'm a glutton or anything—I placed another order, only this one happened entirely inside my own head. I materialized Dana, Willy, Joe, and Emma, as well as Mom, Dad, and Pork Chop (aka Brenda, my little sister).

There was a lot of hugging, high-fives, low-fives, jumping on the bed, and general jubilation. And when I told Joe what I'd ordered from room service, he just about went catatonic on me.

"This sure seems festive, Daniel," said my mom. "What's going on?"

"Attention, everybody," I said, standing on the mahogany credenza and waving at Emma to turn down the sound on the Dance Dance Revolution game she and Pork Chop had begun to play on the room's Wii console.

"As you know, we're once again faced with what some might think is an insurmountable challenge. Not one, but *two* Listers are with us in Tokyo, and all signs suggest that they're about to go critical. What you don't know is that there may actually be *three* of them — they appear to have a son."

"I'm really good with alien kids, you know," said Joe. "Do you think they ever need a sitter?"

"And," I continued, ignoring him, "if that weren't enough, it appears that they might be getting some help from yet another Lister."

"Another in the top ten?!" demanded Dana, putting down her iPhone and looking at me in disgust. "Which one?!"

"Umm," I said, coughing out the answer. "Number 1."

The expressions on their faces ran the emotional spectrum — from Willy's steely defiance to Mom's outright queasiness — but as I dropped that bombshell a uniform look of terror appeared.

"Let's not lose our heads," I said, forcing a smile. I had one more piece of news that I was quite certain none of them would see coming.

"Does anybody know the date?"

"April twenty-ninth," said Joe.

"Not *that* date," I said as the room began to shake and a noise like thunder filled our ears.

Chapter 20

A PARADE OF trumpeting elephants sent us sprawling against the walls amid a confetti storm of flower petals. Never before had anything like this ever been experienced inside the Fujiya Hotel — or, really, anyplace on this side of the planet.

"Gathering Day!" screamed Pork Chop, jumping up and down on the credenza next to me. She was too young to have experienced the last one. To clarify, Alpar Nok, my home planet, circles its sun a little more slowly than Earth does. About twelve times more slowly. So a single Alpar Nokian year is about twelve Earth years long.

You might think maybe this would cause us to have more holidays, but, in fact, we have fewer. So when one happens — and Gathering Day is the biggest of them all — it's a pretty massive thing. Think Christmas, Rosh

Hashanah, Eid ul-Adha, Fourth of July, Bastille Day, Boxing Day, Chinese New Year, Easter, Diwali, Mahavir Jayanti, and your birthday all rolled into one.

My mother dodged an elephant and climbed up next to me with tears in her eyes.

"You remembered, Daniel," she said, so softly I could hardly hear her over the trumpeting pachyderms and, now, the polyphonic strains of the Bryn Spi Philharmonic Orchestra.

Bryn Spi is the capital city, the center of Alpar Nokian culture. It's where the very best of our artists, musicians, and entertainers gather. And, considering that there's never been a nonmusical, nonartistic, nontalented Alpar Nokian, that's saying something.

To hear just one Bryn Spi musician is an amazing thing. To hear a gathering of the hundred best performing the most beautiful and touching piece that has ever been composed, the Departed Symphony, is completely soul lifting. It's a celebration and a remembrance of lost Alpar Nokians—humans and elephants alike. Needless to say, the song got a lot longer after First Strike, the horrible attack on our planet by the Outer Ones that resulted in the decimation of our species.

Legend has it that the symphony is so affecting that it causes people to have visions. Seriously. I don't remember much from my last Gathering Day (when I was a toddler and by then living in Kansas), but they say you can't be exposed to the song and not have an out-of-body experience: seeing dead relatives, conversing with famous Alpar

Nokians from history, or some other grand and enlightening vision.

Within a minute, even tough-as-nails Willy had tears streaming down his face. And I was just starting to go off into la-la land myself. I was beginning to smell the gunjun flowers of my home planet's high mountain plains and was even starting to see a herd of elephants coming toward me—when there was a knock on the door.

I quickly muted the orchestra, hid the parade, and leaped across the room, pressing myself along the wall next to the door.

Everybody was looking to me for some sign. I waved them into defensive positions. It was unlikely to be a noise complaint—I'd of course soundproofed the room so that the noise of this holographic parade wouldn't send hotel management into conniptions—but, then, who could it be? The only certain thing was that the visitor was uninvited.

And, quite possibly, most unwelcome.

Chapter 21

"WHO IS IT?" I asked as innocently as I could.

"It's the Murkamis, Daniel-san," said a voice that sure sounded like Eigi's.

Willy peeked through the keyhole and nodded. I also did a little radar sweep through the door to confirm that there were just four people and that their sizes and shapes matched the Murkamis.

I opened the door and they stepped in, all wearing gleaming Gathering Day robes (made of woven vanadium) and traditional Alpar Nokian headdresses.

"Eigi," I yelled with alarm. "You guys were supposed to have left from Narita Airport by now! It's in the complete opposite direction from here!"

"We're sorry, Daniel-san," he said, bowing contritely.

"But we couldn't leave a fellow Alpar Nokian all alone against those two monsters."

"Besides," said the daughter, Miyu, "you can't exactly show up at the airport in clothes like these and expect to get right on the airplane."

"Yeah," agreed the boy, Kenshin. "Or really go anyplace and expect anybody to think you're not a freak."

"But how did you know we were here?" I asked.

"Dana invited us last night," said Miyu.

"It was kind of obvious they didn't want to leave Tokyo, Daniel," said Dana. "And it seemed wrong not to include them if they were going to be in town. Here, come outside with me."

I waved the Gathering Day parade back into existence for the others and followed Dana outside onto the terrace.

I turned to her in the late-afternoon sunlight. "So how did *you* know I was going to have a Gathering Day party?"

"Well, sometimes, umm, I can kind of read your thoughts."

I looked at her in horror. Could it be true? Because if she could read my thoughts, then she might know when I thought embarrassing things about her, like how I thought she looked really beautiful right then and—

"I mean, not *most* of the time. Just sometimes, when you bring me in and out of existence. Maybe it's because I kind of come out of your mind. It makes sense that sometimes I bump into your thoughts then, you know?" I chuckled self-consciously, and then she continued to torture me by probing my innermost emotions.

75

"Yesterday when you brought us here to check out the GC Headquarters, you were filled with thoughts about Gathering Day. About how you last celebrated it with your parents in Kansas when you were a little boy and how incredible it was. It was really very touching," she said, taking my hand. I turned as red as a lobster in a pot of boiling water.

"I mean," she went on, "you're always thoughtful, Daniel, but thinking of this, remembering this—the loss of your civilization, your family, and the care you give to the others around you, even strangers—"

"Can Willy and the others also see my thoughts sometimes?"

"I don't think so," she guessed.

"That's so weird…" I started to wonder.

"Not as weird as what's about to happen," said a sinister voice just above us.

A massive head peered out over the curving eave of the hotel. The head of a very large insect. A praying mantis, to be precise. A praying mantis with dreadlocks.

"Number 1!!!!" screamed Dana.

Too late. Way too late.

Chapter 22

BEFORE I COULD even flinch, Number 1 had hopped over the edge of the hotel roof and flattened us to the floor of the balcony. And when I say flattened, I don't mean knocked down—I mean *flattened.* Crushed to a thickness of less than an inch.

This wasn't how it was supposed to be. I'd been waiting my whole life to be face-to-face with Number 1, but here it was and there was nothing I could do. I was a pancake...a pancake that was about to become toast. He bent down in my face and mocked me. "Poor little Daniel. Have you been eating enough? You seem so...*thin.*"

He laughed and peeled Dana's crushed body from the balcony floor. She was like a big disk of Play-Doh, all stretched out and wretchedly, helplessly flat. Utter dread seized me. *Was it possible that—*

I couldn't even think it. He'd taken my parents. He couldn't take Dana too.

"Do they play much Frisbee in this country?" Number 1 asked, like I was in any shape to talk. I couldn't even tell where my mouth was except that something tasted gritty and soapy like floor cleaner. Which probably meant at least part of it was against the floor.

He took Dana's flat, motionless body and flung her off the balcony, spinning her out over the trees. How could this be happening? A body couldn't possibly survive in this shape. If he'd crushed us, he'd crushed us, right? Dana must be dead. I must be dead. I must be—

"Getting your bearings back, little Alien Hunter?" Number 1 asked, bending down, his bug eyes flashing red. "Starting to figure it all out, are you?"

Now he started to peel *me* off the floor. Was he going to toss me off the balcony too? Would I land near Dana's body?

He was laughing. "I guess I was right not to adjust my schedule and deal with you before now. You're obviously not as adept a hunter as either of your parents were. By your age, each of them was more formidable than you are. And, clearly, even the two of them never became a true threat, not *really*."

He held me out in front of him and looked into my flattened eyes.

"Still," he seethed, "there's no sense taking unnecessary risks."

And, with that, he extended his disgusting insect jaws,

clamped them onto to me, and began to *blow*. He was filling me with foul alien breath! *He was inflating me.*

It was too disgusting to even contemplate, but my limbs and head started to regain their accustomed shape, and then—

Suddenly, I was standing on the balcony again with a nonflat Dana. My friends, the Murkamis, and my family were still inside watching the Gathering Day parade of elephants, listening to the orchestra.

Had that entire weird scene with Number 1 been just a Gathering Day vision?

I grabbed Dana's hand to make sure she was real. She was.

I never wanted to let go.

Chapter 23

THE GATHERING DAY party went on later than it should have—especially on a weeknight—but there wasn't really anybody to blame but myself. After all, no one was forcing me to wake up at 6 a.m. to try on Japanese school uniforms.

Staring at myself in the bedroom mirror, I decided that—except for the bags under my eyes—I basically looked like Little Lord Fancypants. Almost every school in Japan requires kids to wear *seifuku*, and like most uniforms, they aren't exactly, um, hip. I understood the purpose behind them—I'm sure they helped to keep students from getting distracted with superficial concerns—but the one I was wearing right then made me look like a cross between an admiral and a theme-park greeter.

It was a good thing I'd gotten the Murkamis their own room and that my friends and family weren't around right then, or I'm sure I'd have never heard the end of it. Of course, they probably wouldn't have approved of my plan, either. I confess. I knew it wasn't the safest thing in the world to be interfering in the hunt of the last living Pleionid in the universe.

Using my List computer, I'd done some refresher research on the legendary species. Pleionids had been unique in all the universe for their unsurpassed ability to change shape and color (kind of like me, but with *way* more options). Their gift was enabled by a compound called pleiochromatech that was so chemically complicated and unstable that it had never been successfully duplicated in any laboratory.

And that was what had caused the species' downfall. Ever notice how the rarer a thing is, the more valuable it becomes? Well, pleiochromatech—despite the fact that nobody ever even figured out how it worked—at one point was worth more per milligram than pure lawrencium, and that meant that every unscrupulous merchant in the cosmos was paying top dollar for the stuff. So it wasn't long after the Pleionid's home planet was discovered that entire armies of poachers descended and all but wiped them out.

A handful had been rescued by well-meaning agents of the Federation of Outer Ones and sequestered in "safe houses" around the universe, but, one by one, the few survivors had died of natural causes or had been hunted down. Speaking as a member of another decimated species, I had some sense for how hard it is to persevere under such circumstances.

But I also knew other things about the mind-set of a survivor. And I wondered if this last Pleionid might be willing to help prevent the same fate from befalling another innocent species—aka you humans. Plus, The Prayer had ordered Number 7 and Number 8 to keep the Pleionid away from me at all costs, so there must be something we could do to help each other.

I slung my book bag over my shoulder, adjusted my uniform's crisp lapels, and headed outside to join the similarly dressed schoolchildren of Japan. My mission? To befriend the son of Number 7 and Number 8.

I had a sneaking suspicion we had at least one enemy in common.

Chapter 24

WHEN IT COMES to schools and children, Japanese culture is pretty serious. We're talking proper terms of respect for teachers (sensei), loudspeaker announcements alerting the public to use caution when students are headed to and from school, and meticulous attention to students' safety while they're at school too.

Which meant that even with a perfectly tailored uniform and the universe's most pleasant demeanor, I wasn't going to be able to just march into Kildare's school and sit at the desk next to him.

It was a little exhausting, but I basically had to brainwash my way into Kildare's class. From the first group of kids I bumped into on the sidewalk to the crossing guard to the homeroom teacher—I mentally created for each of them the impression that I was somebody they knew, somebody they shouldn't be suspicious of or throw off the premises.

It's easier done than explained in this case—human psychology isn't the easiest thing to understand, much less manipulate—but Mom had given me a smattering of psychological operations training, and somehow I managed to pull it off.

Just being let into the school wasn't enough; I still had to find Kildare. I'd hacked into the school server and swiped his class schedule, but he wasn't in the classroom it indicated he'd be in. I wandered the hallways, peering into classrooms, checking the playground, the music rooms, the cafeteria, and then, as I made my way past the gymnasium, I heard a bunch of boys laughing and taunting somebody.

That's when I first saw him, standing without a shred of resistance in front of five mean-looking boys. One of them, the spiky-haired ringleader, gave Kildare a push that sent him spinning into a wood-and-glass display case that lined the wall. I suppressed the urge to put an end to this unfair fight, but it wasn't easy. If there's one thing that never fails to tick me off, it's bullies.

But this kid they were shoving around was the child of the most powerful alien couple I'd ever encountered. And something told me, if push came to shove, he'd be able to take care of himself.

I slunk back out of sight and watched the scene from around the corner.

"You going to give us your homework, bug boy?" asked the ringleader.

"Of course, Ichi," replied Kildare without a trace of sarcasm or defiance. He produced a notebook from his bag. "You want me to copy it into your notebooks for you?"

"In *your* handwriting? Then the teacher would know it isn't ours, stupid," he barked, shoving Kildare harder this time.

I again fought the urge to go over and kick their butts and stayed out of sight where I was.

"Get that garbage can," the ringleader said, gesturing to a round plastic trash barrel just down the hall. Two of the little brutes got the can. And the next thing I knew, the five of them had taken Kildare's book bag, thrown it in the garbage, and shoved him, butt-first, into the can. He was wedged so far in that the crooks of his knees hung over one side and his armpits over another.

"Now put him up there," commanded the leader, pointing to the top of the trophy case. His hench-bullies looked at each other quizzically, and first one, then all of them started to laugh.

"Quickly!" the leader urged. They stopped laughing and hoisted the garbage can—with Kildare in it—atop the trophy case.

Then they fled down the hallway, one of them yelling, "Hey, somebody needs to take out the trash down here!"

With little choice but to wait for a janitor to discover him, Kildare was in quite a pickle. He could probably have toppled the can over by rocking his weight back and forth, but if he did that he'd plummet at least six feet to the concrete floor and might land on his head. Seriously, I couldn't envision any other way he could unwedge himself from the can. The human body has limitations, and extricating one from a round plastic waste barrel into which it has been forced butt-first is a biggie.

But he *wasn't* human, was he?

Why had he let a bunch of bullies do this to him? And why was he just sitting up there, slowly counting backward to himself in Japanese, "*Ju, kyu, hachi, shichi, roku, go, shi, san, ni, ichi*—"

When he reached zero, he drew a breath and—mindfreak—turned *gray* and then dissolved into little tiny particles. At least that's what it looked like to me.

I don't think I actually said "Holy frijoles!" out loud, but I must have inhaled or something, because his color and former shape instantly returned and his head swiveled toward me, his piercing dark eyes locking on mine as a chill shot up my spine.

"Who *are* you!?" he wanted to know.

Chapter 25

ACTUALLY, HIS TONE was probably more embarrassed than threatening. I didn't feel so much scared as I did guilty—like I'd just seen something that I probably shouldn't have, like I'd been spying on him. Which, I guess, I had.

There was no way I could use my human-tested Jedi mind trick to convince him I was just another human kid who'd been enrolled here for the past two years. Other than the fact that he seemed to have a superhuman tolerance for bullies, I knew next to nothing about how his alien mind might work. Chances were, if I tried to interfere with his thoughts, the only thing I'd end up doing would be flagging myself as a fellow alien.

So instead, I reached into my bag of superpowers and

pulled out my most tried-and-true paranormal ability—playing stupid.

"Uh, hi! Like, I'm Daniel. Who are you?"

"I'm Kildare Gygax. Nice to meet you, Daniel. Want to do me a favor and see if you can help me down from here? There should be a stepladder in the janitor's closet down the hall over there."

"How do you know that?"

"Let's just say this isn't the first time something like this has happened to me."

"Those bullies have stuck you up there in a garbage can before?"

"Actually, last time they hung me by my underpants on a climbing peg halfway up the gymnasium wall. But the stepladder was helpful then too."

"That's terrible," I said, grimacing at the thought. "Shouldn't I go get a teacher?"

"And then have said teacher ask me what happened, and have to implicate Ichi or one of his thugs—or pin the blame on somebody innocent—and deal with all the repercussions of that? No, thank you."

"But if you don't, you're just giving in to those bullies!" I blurted.

He looked at me with a mixture of pity and impatience.

"As I'm sure you know, Daniel, there's a long history of bullying in high schools. And Japan's no exception. In fact, some statistics say we've got the worst juvenile bullying culture on earth."

I found that hard to believe. The population seemed so . . . mild mannered. "Really?"

"Really," he said. "Now, seriously, I'm losing feeling in my feet."

"I'll go get that ladder," I said, and went to retrieve it.

"So," he said after I came back, as I climbed up and somehow managed to help him out of the can without killing us both. "What's another gaijin doing in this place?"

"Umm, I just transferred. Parents moved here for work."

"What do they do?"

"Um," I said, suddenly realizing there was a danger in seeming *too* stupid. "They, um, handle personnel training for a nongovernmental organization."

"Oh," he said. "Well, I didn't think I'd seen you before."

"Yeah, well," I said, "it's not like I tend to make a big impression on people anyway."

"Just the fact that you're talking to me is all the impression I need," Kildare said, fishing his book bag out of the bottom of the trash barrel. He put it on his back and made the weirdest noise — it was a like a cross between a sneeze and a cat's purr.

"Odaiji ni," I said.

"What?!"

"It means 'bless you' — you know, what you say when somebody sneezes."

"I didn't sneeze," he said, starting to turn red.

"Oh," I said, not quite sure how to respond.

"Anyhow, thanks for the help."

"You're welcome," I said, meaning it quite sincerely. Other than making weird sneezing noises and then denying them, he seemed like a nice, grounded kid. I mean, I wasn't exactly going to let my guard down to a child of two top-ten List aliens, but...

"Say, what class do you have next?" I asked.

"Introductory zoology," he said.

"Really?" I said, whipping out a class schedule and pretending to read the same course. "Me, too. Can you show me where it is?"

"Sure," he said. "But I suggest you not walk in with me. Ichi's in that class. In fact, that's kind of why he and his friends stuck me in the garbage can. They wanted to borrow my homework."

"'Borrow,' huh?" I said.

"Yeah, well, there are worse things," he said.

"Like what?"

"Well, if you're still intent on coming to class with me, I'm sure you'll see them do something worse than that. They're especially rough on new kids."

Chapter 26

"*CELASTRINA ARGIOLUS, GLAUCOPSYCHE alexis, Vanessa atalanta, Gonepteryx cleopatra, Hesperia comma, Inachis io, Lysandra bellargus, Quercusia quercus,* and *Danaus plexippus.*"

"Very good, Mr. Gygax," said Professor Kuniyoshi, beaming with pride at his star pupil's recitation.

You know how some kids get geeky about computers or writing or drama or history or music? Well, for Kildare, science class seemed to be his thing. Big time.

When old Professor Kuniyoshi unstacked and displayed his enormous butterfly collection—after telling a long rambling story about how he'd been all over the world to obtain it—most of the students looked bored and on the verge of unconsciousness. But Kildare looked like a little kid on Christmas morning. And, when asked to identify the specimens, he recited their scientific names with something close to bliss.

Which was a pretty bold move, since we all know that if there's one truth about bullies the world over, it's that nothing sets them off like other people's happiness. So, as Kildare boiled over with geeky enthusiasm, Ichi began to boil over with malignant intent.

Ichi was a compact, muscle-bound kid with a face that seemed to know only two expressions: snarling resentment (which he wore when adults were looking), and belligerent disdain (which he wore when kids were looking). Right then, safely in the back of the room and sitting behind a tall kid so that Professor Kuniyoshi couldn't see him, he was wearing the latter. And he was drawing back a very thick rubber band to which he'd fastened a metal paper clip.

Thwak!

Professor Kuniyoshi stopped talking and turned around at the noise but—not noticing the paper-clipped rubber band on the floor behind Kildare, or the tear trickling out of Kildare's eye, or Ichi's friends' barely suppressed laughter—turned back to the board and continued to draw the common elements of moth wings.

Kildare looked like he was just going to suck up the pain. I, however, had reached my breaking point. I was going to teach this bully a lesson about entomology.

I turned my attention to the hundreds of butterflies and moths on their display mounts on the table in front of Professor Kuniyoshi. Then with my mind I popped the pins from their wings and *brought them back from the dead*.

First one, then another, then every single specimen in the collection twitched, quivered, fluttered, and flew up into the air.

The entire class sat up and watched, openmouthed, as the butterflies gathered in an enormous colorful cloud in the middle of the room.

And then, en masse, they streaked to the back of the class and began to dive-bomb Ichi's spiky-haired head.

"Ah-ah-ah-ah!" screamed Ichi in a voice so piercing and panicked he sounded more like a seven-year-old girl than a fourteen-year-old thug. "Get them off!!"

He leaped from his chair, swatting wildly about his head.

This time when poor Professor Kuniyoshi turned around, he didn't fail to notice what was happening. But he didn't quite know what to do about it.

"My collection?" He gasped. "My butterflies? Ichi, what are you doing to my butterflies?! Don't you dare harm my specimens, young man!"

"Get them off me!" shrieked Ichi, running laps around the room now. They weren't really hurting him, of course, but Ichi was apparently scared enough to fear the worst.

The rest of the class, including Ichi's so-called friends, were roaring with laughter. Everybody, that is, except for Kildare, who had turned around in his seat and was *staring right at me*.

93

Chapter 27

SCHOOL IS *EXHAUSTING*. I don't know how human kids do it. By the time I got back to the suite, I could barely stand up. I wasn't even going to change out of my dorky sailor-boy *seifuku*. I was just going to let myself in, unsling my book bag, and sleep on the nearest soft object I could find—a couch, a bed, an area rug, a pile of clothes…

But no sooner had I opened the door and stepped inside than—WHAM!—I was facedown on the bamboo floor with my arm twisted behind my back and the whining sound of a fully charged Opus 24/24 in my ear.

My powerful assailant's weight shifted, driving a knee into the small of my back.

"You could be dead right now, Daniel," whispered a voice I knew all too well, a voice I should have known to expect at just a moment such as this.

"Dad, I've had a rough day. Can you *please* let me up?"

"You expect to take on Number 7, Number 8, *and* Number 1, and you walk blindly into your hotel room without running a security sweep? Have you forgotten everything you've been taught?"

"Dad," I pleaded, "my arm, my—"

Dad let go of my wrist and got up, but he didn't power down the Opus 24/24.

Opus 24/24s have only one setting—eternal damnation. They contain an illegal molecular resonator that fires a gigawatt pulse that vibrates at the precise frequency of its victim's neurotransmissions. In the simplest terms, it causes its victims to expire from pure *pain*. Which is kind of why they're banned across most of the civilized universe.

Seeing one in my father's hands was a little jarring to say the least. It was the very same weapon The Prayer had used to kill him and my mother.

"Dad, put that thing down already, okay?"

"*Make* me," he commanded in a voice that sent chills down my spine. He was challenging me as part of our ongoing training exercises, but I don't think he realized how truly exhausted I was.

Just as I was about to tell him he was seconds away from being dematerialized—stored in the lower levels of my consciousness until I needed him again—he grabbed me with one hand and flung me across the room into a Noguchi glass coffee table, which promptly shattered.

"Ouch. What the *heck?!*"

I struggled to my feet, anger boiling inside me. It was

one thing to keep me on my toes, but it was another to take advantage of a tired kid who'd already had a pretty rough day.

"Look, Dad. That wasn't funny, and—"

"You might want to dive through, Daniel," he suggested.

"Dive through? What's that supposed to mean?"

By way of reply, he deftly aimed the Opus 24/24 at me and squeezed the trigger.

Chapter 28

WAIT A SECOND, I thought. *Actually, wait a* whole bunch *of seconds.*

Though my recollection is hazy at best, when I was just two—and he was still alive—my father had taught me how it's possible to *dive through* the surface of time.

It's something I recently pulled off while in the grips of a man-eating space anemone that had disguised itself as a van. And of course there was that time I managed to put myself back quite a few centuries, all the way to the time of King Arthur...

Anyhow, I'm not good at explaining the physics of the time-travel process, but suffice it to say it's pretty taxing. The power to dive through the current, the fabric of the here and now, comes straight out of your emotions. So you've got to be really riled up when you do it. Freaked out about something like, oh, say, your father firing the cruelest weapon ever created *right at your head.*

Even as the Opus 24/24 discharged—a plasma pulse of pure pain erupting from its wicked, sawtooth muzzle—I dove through the space-time continuum and put the entire situation on standby.

It's pretty intense, really, to have everything in the world suddenly stop and hang in the air like you're walking around in a museum diorama. Intense, but also a little lonely, and *quiet* like you wouldn't believe.

"Very good, Daniel," my father said stepping back from the still-frozen Opus 24/24. "But what do you do if your *opponent* is also able to manipulate time?" He walked around the floating weapon, as if to emphasize his point.

"Look, Dad. It's one thing to give me fighting tips and keep me on my guard and all that, but I need some rest right now. I'll have you over after I've taken a nap, okay?"

"You're not answering my question, Daniel. Do you know for certain that Number 7 or Number 8 can't stop time?"

"No. I mean, we know almost nothing about them, but I don't think—"

"Oh, you *don't think?*" he said mockingly, waving his arms and somehow casting us both backward in time, slowly at first, and then faster, faster, faster.

In a blink, we were watching my arrival at the hotel, and then the guest before me, a businessman of some sort, and then back to the one before that, and the one before that and then—*bam!*—there were soldiers around. American soldiers. And there was some military dude I recognized in khakis smoking a corncob pipe. General Douglas MacArthur? The man who'd been entrusted with Japan's recovery after World War II and had helped start the nation on one of the world's most remarkable comebacks of all time.

I could have yelled hello, but then—*bam!*—the hotel was being built, and we were hovering in the air over the horses and carts of the nineteenth-century construction crew, and then—*bam!*—we were hovering over the previous building on the site, maybe a hotel too but shorter? and then—*bam!*—we were back back to when the site was occupied by a small, curved-roof house and there was a big stone castle not far away. Just then the earth started to shake. I looked off in the distance and saw a huge black cloud exploding out of Mount Fuji—it must be the famous eruption of 1707!

Before I could scramble for cover—*bam!*—we were at a camp of ancient Japanese soldiers armed with wooden spears and polished stone axes, and then—*bam!*—back to pristine forest. And then—*bam!*—back to some sort of ice age and we were on a glacier, and then the glacier was gone and there was a grassland, and then a forest with really weird trees, and then—

"This should do," said my father, looking around at the primitive jungle. "So, Daniel, it's time you got caught up on your homework. What do you know for a fact about Number 7 and Number 8?"

"They run a video-game company, live in Tokyo, have a son, a really nice apartment, and they like to hunt and eat endangered aliens?"

"So what puts them in the List's top ten?"

"They're plotting to decimate the human race by brainwashing kids to become killing machines like the ones in their video games."

"You mean to go after them, and *this* is all you know? What's the rest of their plan? How will they initiate it? How do you know it hasn't already begun?"

"Well—" I started to say, but I knew he was right. Had I ever been this badly underprepared for anything?

"And how about Number 1?" he asked me. "We've heard he's been in town recently. What have you learned about him after all these years on the same planet with him?"

"You mean other than that he can give a person bad nightmares?"

"What do you know about him in terms of his abilities or physical appearances—"

"Well, he has dreadlocks, red bug eyes, looks like a big giant praying mantis—"

"Always?"

"Well, the List computer says he's a shape-shifter—"

"So, he could, in theory, look like *this?*" asked my father, morphing into a twenty-foot-tall carnivorous dinosaur with red bug eyes and dreadlocks.

"Run, Daniel. *Run*," he roared.

I didn't ask. I just did.

Chapter **29**

I GUESS YOU'VE got to trust your parents know what's best for you. Even when they're in the form of the largest land-based predator the Earth's ever known and are testing your ability to survive by attempting to *kill* you.

"Daniel," boomed my tyrannosaur father, knocking down a huge fern tree as he charged after me. "Here are the rules to this little training exercise—" He cut himself short to lunge at me with his wicked six-inch teeth. I barely managed to leap over a moss-covered boulder and out of reach.

"Each time you survive one of my attempts on your life, you earn a catechism question."

"What kind of reward is *that?!*" I panted.

My dad was big into what he called his "catechism"—a way of verbally instructing me with hard-core questions on all manner of philosophical and ethical topics.

"And each correctly answered question—" he roared, stubbing one of his big clawed toes on a spiky cycad plant, "will earn you the next level. Complete all the levels, and today's training will be complete."

"And if I don't complete all the levels?"

"You ever wonder what it would be like to get bitten in half?" he said, stopping and snapping his enormous jaws down at me.

I leaped out of the way and took off in a new direction.

"Okay," he bellowed. "First catechism question: Give me a Japanese proverb on the subject of the difference between wisdom and memory."

I *knew* this one: "Knowledge without wisdom is a load of books on the back of an, um, donkey." Call me crazy, but even if my dad was conjured up by my own mind, I wasn't fond of using what my mother would call "coarse" language around him.

"I trust you can see how the saying applies to your current situation."

I didn't have a chance to think it through right then. *Bam!* Dad was now back as his usual self, and we were standing in the future—*way* in the future by the looks of it. We were in some sort of high-tech, robot-operated assembly plant with silver Honda logos all over the place. Laser saws, titanium rivet guns, and ceramic shears were slicing, dicing, puncturing, folding, and hammering large shapes out of metal, carbon fiber, glass, and plastic all around us.

This was clearly a place for machines, not people. The

air was stifling hot and smelled of sulfur, but worse than the air was the noise. *Deafening* is too weak a word. It felt like hammers landing on the sides of my head. It was too loud to do anything, much less think, and I almost didn't notice Dad leveling the Opus 24/24 at me again.

I leaped backward, landing on a high-speed conveyor belt as the blast ricocheted off a junction box and hit an assembly robot. The poor thing actually seemed to scream as it burst into a thousand pieces.

I smiled triumphantly back at my father.

I couldn't hear him, but it was easy enough to read his lips: "You only earn a question when you *survive!*" was what he said.

I rolled over just in time to notice I was being whisked into an enormous laser cutter.

I thought quickly. I knew from my studies that lasers are made of light and therefore will pass harmlessly through anything that's perfectly clear. I rearranged my molecules to be transparent to visible radiation, and, sure enough, I passed through the machine and emerged on the other side entirely intact—well, except for my book bag, which I'd kind of forgotten to make invisible with the rest of me.

I swiftly hopped off the conveyor belt and flung the flaming thing to the ground before it burned my back. At least my teachers wouldn't have to hear that the dog ate my homework.

Suddenly, the machines stopped and quiet returned, except for the ringing in my ears. Dad had paused time once again.

"Congratulations," he said. "You've earned yourself another question. Ready?"

I nodded wearily.

"Who said, 'Success is 99 percent failure'?"

My mind was blank. I was thinking it was somebody Japanese, but—

"Answer the question, Daniel, or if you'd rather, we can play this level again."

I racked my brains and did a quick search through the virtual Wikipedia I'd installed in my head. "Um," I said, playing it cool, so Dad didn't discover I had kind of, sort of, cheated. "Soichiro Honda, the guy who started the manufacturing company."

"And I trust you see why that, too, is applicable to your current situation."

"You mean I should assume Number 1's going to have some serious failures coming soon because he's had 99 percent successes so far?"

"I'm saying you can profit from your mistakes."

"Ah," I said, not following him, but once again not exactly having enough time to speculate. Because now I was standing on what looked to be a near present-day Tokyo street. Judging by the big white-and-orange concrete barriers lining it, it looked like it was closed off for a Grand Prix street-race course.

"Next question," Dad continued. "What two words did General MacArthur, supreme commander of Japan in the years after World War II, say summed up the history of failure in war?"

This one I knew all too well.

"Too late," I said.

Dad nodded and was gone.

My ears were still ringing from the car factory, but I detected a sort of roaring, thunder-like sound in the distance. And it was getting louder by the second.

Chapter 30

IT WAS NOT a mystery that took long to figure out. In a moment, I saw the source of the noise—*motorcycles*—1400cc Hondas, in all poetic probability.

Dear Old Dad had transported me right into the middle of a MotoGP exhibition street course in downtown Tokyo. A pack of overpowered, smooth-tired street racers was now rounding the corner about a half mile away and coming straight at me. They'd have plenty of time to stop or steer around me, assuming they took pity on me.

But it was soon obvious, mainly from how they were laughing and pointing, that they had no interest in avoiding me. The fact that the racers were barb-tailed, cloven-hoofed, red-horned *demons*—or, at least, a species of alien that very much looked that way—was also something of a warning sign.

Fortunately, the course was less than one hundred and fifty feet wide, so I didn't need to sprint much faster than Usein Bolt to get to safety. When I glanced back at them from the side of the road, it looked like they didn't care I was escaping. They were still speeding forward and laughing their pointy heads off.

I turned to see what they were looking at and spotted their *real* target: a little girl clutching a big Hello Kitty doll and frozen in pure horror at the sight of the approaching demon bikers.

"RUN!" I screamed, skidding to a stop at the barrier. This would be close — the demons were about to go by me, and the girl wasn't much farther. If I was going to save her, there weren't even seconds —

Time-out! If I could stop time, but I knew immediately I couldn't dive below the surface right then. It's one of those things you either can or can't feel, and I definitely didn't have the feeling.

So I did the next best thing. In an instant, I gauged the distance, studied the ground by her side, and teleported myself there.

"Grab hold of me!" I yelled

Teleporting others is not a good idea unless you happen to know the location and nature of every molecule in their bodies, because if you make any bad assumptions, well... just be sure to bring a bucket and a mop.

So that meant right then I had somewhere on the order of 1.043 seconds in which to physically carry her out of harm's way.

She started to grab me as I turned and glanced into the yellows of the approaching demons' loathsome eyes. I quickly calculated the leap I was going to have to make to get us airborne and to safety. But there was something wrong with how she was holding on to me—something *painfully* wrong. I turned to look at her and saw what it was.

She was no longer a cute little girl with a cute little stuffed animal in her arms; she was a long-tailed, red-skinned demon—a demon with very sharp teeth that she had just sunk into my left arm. The pain was beyond anything I'd ever experienced. To complicate matters, the Hello Kitty doll had grown an evil monobrow and six-inch-long claws that it was using to climb up my back, probably so it could slice my throat.

Time seemed to slow, and all the panicked stretched-out split-seconds made me realize that, aside from the raging pain of being bitten and clawed, (a) I could no longer leap clear of the oncoming motorcycles, at least without leaving my arm behind, and (b) I was about to become 110 pounds of alien roadkill.

I was about to die.

I couldn't believe it. I'd come this far and then, just like that, it was the end.

Only, of course, it wasn't exactly.

The scene disappeared, and I was back in my deluxe suite at the Fujiya Hotel with Dad.

"Daniel," said Dad in a sad voice, "if this training exercise had been a test at school, you would have received a forty-seven point four out of a hundred. In other words, an F. It's entirely clear that you can't possibly win against Number 7 and Number 8 right now, much less with Number 1 in the picture. You should leave Japan. Immediately."

"But I can dive back through time and take it again, can't I?"

He shook his head. "No. No, you can't, Daniel. These training exercises are all in your mind. You'll see that if you try it in real life, you won't be able to. Since your last adventure, Number 1 has put a disruption field over the entire planet."

"What the heck does that mean?" I asked, suddenly remembering what Number 1 had told Number 7 and Number 8.

"It means you couldn't time-travel if you tried."

"I don't believe you!" I said, and tried to visualize the surface of time so I could dive through. I was going to jump back thirty seconds, just to prove my point; but I couldn't see it! Everything was gray and filled with static, like an old TV set when you don't have a good signal.

"You see?" asked my father. "Leave Japan, Daniel. There's no hope for you this time."

"I can do it anyway," I insisted.

But there was nobody there to hear me. Dad was gone.

Chapter 31

YOU KNOW WHO wins in a fight between Exhausted and Stressed Out? Yeah, Stressed Out. I not only didn't pass that all-night test with Dad; I managed to fail it with flaming colors.

I decided against taking a much-needed nap and soon found myself standing a block away from the GC Tower, contemplating the best way to get inside and do some more spying on Number 7 and Number 8. My window-washing gig had worked out okay, but it definitely had certain drawbacks. Like the fact that if they didn't happen to be in a penthouse with floor-to-ceiling windows, I'd have no idea what they were up to.

I didn't have much time to rig up the window-washing

gondola now anyway. If there was one thing Dad's test had done—besides making me even more tired—it had proved that I needed to become better prepared—and fast. I needed to learn *everything* I could about these two. I needed *unlimited access*.

I considered a few options. In theory I could make myself into a computer virus and infect the building's security systems, hacking into the cameras and microphones they had doubtless installed throughout the facility. But that was probably too risky. Although I'd been doing a lot of research on digital information systems lately, I hadn't actually tried to be a computer program before, and, judging by Number 7 and Number 8's success with their video games, their digital security would probably be light-years better than anything Earth had ever seen.

I also considered disguising myself as a security guard again. But this time I was going to be among top-ten List aliens, and it was highly unlikely I'd be able to bluster or brainwash my way past them.

No, if I really wanted to be a fly on the wall, the best thing to do was to make myself into a creature as common to Japan as it is the United States: *Musca domestica,* the ubiquitous housefly. One with a miniaturized Alien Hunter brain in its tiny head.

When nobody was looking, I transformed myself and flew over to the uniformed shoulder of a passing teenage boy who, sure enough, was headed straight into the GC flagship store for an early-morning video-game session before heading off to school.

Now I just needed to hope that Number 7 and Number 8 weren't as high-tech with the building's pest control as they were about other things.

Chapter 32

TWENTY THOUSAND HIGH-RANKING alien thugs were making their way through the building's lobby. Well, that's how it looked through fly eyes anyhow. It took me a moment to get used to my new senses and to realize there were just a dozen of them. Still, that was a lot.

I flew as fast as I could to catch up and landed on the hat of the tallest one, just as a security guard waved him through the turnstile.

My steed and his buddies then crammed into a single elevator that shot us up to the fifty-first floor where we entered a conference room whose walls were lined with alien antlers, bones, stuffed heads, pelts, and other hunting trophies. The conference table also looked to be from some sort of creature— the hip bone of an enormous animal. And, by "enormous," I mean the bone must have been at least a hundred feet long and thirty feet wide. When intact, the actual creature was probably big enough to accidentally inhale a city bus.

The aliens took their seats around the table, and the meeting was called to order.

Number 7 presided from the head of the table as the thugs took off their human disguises. The hat I was riding was unceremoniously tossed to the middle of the table, and, unfortunately for me, it didn't have ribbons or feathers or anything I could use for cover. I was totally out in the open. My only defense was to stay perfectly still. Fortunately, for the moment, nobody seemed to notice the little black fleck on the brim of the gray hat.

"As you know," began Number 7, "today marks the launch of a new level. It will be the most challenging— and rewarding—hunt you've ever undertaken."

He had them all on the hook, and he knew it.

"What is it?" demanded one of them. "A Mahoneyian Stinkbear?"

"A Corruscated Fosterite?"

"An Endomorphic Nebulan?"

"A Pleionid," replied Number 7, cutting short the welter of speculation as if he'd fired a gunshot.

The thugs straightened in their chairs and went wide-eyed, or, if they didn't have eyes, widened other things.

"But—" began the tall one I'd ridden in on.

"No, they're *not* quite extinct," said Number 7. "There's one left. And it's here—here in Japan."

The hunters looked like they were about to break into applause, but Number 7 would have none of it.

"The mission brief, which I'll feed into your consoles at sundown, will contain a link to the creature's location. Because of its shape-shifting and self-healing abilities, we couldn't use a traditional transponder. Nevertheless, we have another way to track the creature that will allow us to send you rough coordinates."

A murmur of speculation rippled through the room. I too wondered how they might be tracking the Pleionid.

"Also," said Number 7, glancing at Number 8, "to make things even more challenging, a new hunter will join us tonight, a truly formidable competitor."

"Who is it? Is he here?" asked one of the hunters.

"You'll see."

"This sounds like a tough assignment," said another. "Are there any special incentives?"

"First of all," said Number 7, standing to his full height and briefly, somehow, turning a disturbing shade of gray, "this is not an *assignment*. This is a *hunt*. All of you signed up for this. But, yes, if you like to think in terms of what's in it for you, I can tell you that whoever successfully kills the Pleionid"—he paused dramatically—"not only gets the trophy, but *gets to live*."

Now it was every other alien in the room's opportunity to turn gray.

"You mean—?" began one of them, an owl-headed goon with eyes like mirrored lawn balls.

"I should clarify," continued Number 7. "Because of your miserable failure with the Mahlerian bird-cat, it has been decided to thin your ranks and recruit new players. Those of you who fail to bring down the Pleionid will be *terminated*."

Another ripple of shock and surprise rounded the room, but not as quickly as I would have expected in a group that was just told they were about to die. One of them, with a face like a giant squirrel—if the squirrel didn't have any hair on its face (*very* creepy)—was even smirking.

"I don't care. I've been getting pretty tired of this game," he said.

Number 7 smiled. "What, you mean this 5G edition of Intergalactic Safari Hunter?"

"Duh," said the creepy squirrel.

"Do you know what '5G' means?"

"Fifth Generation," said the owl-headed goon. "It's a marketing thing to make it sound advanced, right?"

"Actually, it's a number we developers use to indicate the final phase of a video-game arc. Previous generations of the program entice players to continue, thereby helping us to optimize programming to ensure we have maximized its addictive properties.

"For instance, with the humans, right now we're up to the 4G version. The next edition will be the 5G, just like yours."

"So?" said the freaky squirrel.

"So," said Number 7, "at 5G, it stops being a game. And

when we release that edition here—as we've done on several planets before, including your own—all the world's gamers are going to start acting out the ultraviolent competitions we lay before them in *real* life."

So that was how they were going to make humans extinct. They were going to turn all the first-person shooting and war games into the real thing. The game players of the world would go berserk across the planet.

"What does that mean for us?" asked the owl-headed one.

"Have you tried to pause the game lately? Tried to get up from your machine and go get a snack?"

The aliens looked a degree more nervous. Some of them nodded gloomily.

"You see, now you are not playing Intergalactic Safari Hunter. You are *living* it. This is not your video-game self—this is your *real* self. In other words, no more restarting the level if you happen to die."

You could almost hear the sickening realizations dawn around the boardroom table. This was why they hadn't been able to pause the game. This was why everything had seemed so real. And this was why Number 7's threat to terminate them should be taken seriously.

I wasn't sure what kind of a long-term management technique it was, but something told me that Number 7 had just lit quite a motivating little fire under these greedy, selfish aliens, and that this night's hunt was going to be particularly hard fought.

That poor Pleionid didn't stand a snowball's chance in hell, whatever its abilities were. I cleaned my eyes and flicked my wings, which I guess is the fly equivalent of a discouraged head shake.

"How disgusting!" screeched Number 8. "A fly! There on that hat! Somebody vaporize it!"

Uh-oh.

Chapter 33

I ZIGGED, I zagged, I climbed, I dove, and somehow I actually managed to dodge a half dozen swipes from hands, claws, tentacles, and even several blasts from a variety of alien weapons.

Being small, fast, and nimble was a huge advantage. Fortunately, such an accomplished gathering of intergalactic safari hunters was used to going after larger and more interesting prey, and somehow I made it away from the conference table, and then under the door, and then out into the hallway, without any of them in hot pursuit.

Still, next time I tried spying as a fly and found myself in the middle of a table surrounded by alien safari hunters, I resolved to do a better job blending in.

I landed on the ceiling a little way down the hall and tried to recover my fly breath, but a moment later the conference-room doors burst open and the aliens poured out, readjusting their human costumes and grumbling like a bunch of high-school students who'd just been given five hours of homework.

"I can't believe this," whined one of them.

"Should we just take those two out and run the hunt ourselves?" suggested another.

"Yeah, you give that a try. They didn't get top-ten rankings for nothing."

"Maybe we should just get the heck out of here."

"Great idea," another chimed in. "Let's all just leave this backwater planet."

"I mean, if we don't *try* to hunt the Pleionid, then we can't *fail*, right? And, if we don't fail, they won't terminate us."

"Yeah, seriously, that's a great idea! We know it's not a game now, right? So we just need to get away!"

"Hey, wait a second. What guarantee do any of us have that we'd *all* leave? I mean, how would I know if you decide to stay? This hunt would be pretty easy to win if there was just one guy in it."

"I'd never go back on my word..."

"You're so full of it. That's it; I'm staying right here. You guys couldn't hunt your way out of a paper bag anyway."

I guessed Number 7 and Number 8 knew a thing or two about the psychological makeups of these selfish hunters. There was no way they would abandon this opportunity to hunt one of the universe's most legendary creatures if it meant letting somebody else have the chance.

I dropped back onto my favorite hat and rode it down to the lobby.

The aliens exited the building together, but as soon as they'd stepped out into the bright Tokyo morning, they all took off in different directions. Mine, after checking to make sure nobody was following him, crossed the plaza and loped down the avenue to a noodle shop just a block away from the big Japanese Rail train station.

I'm not usually a soup fanatic, but I guess my fly senses were tuned a little differently than my regular ones. As it was, the place smelled so good I almost drowned in my own fly drool, and it was only through an act of sheer will that I kept my wits about me and resisted the temptation to dive-bomb somebody's udon noodles.

I kept looking around the narrow restaurant, expecting to pick out another alien in the crowd, but everyone seemed to be distinctly human. Everyone, that is, except for the counter girl who soon came to take my alien's order.

"*Dana!?*" I squeaked.

Fortunately, I was a fly, and nobody could hear me.

Chapter 34

"WHAT CAN I get you, sir?" asked Dana, passing my alien a moist washcloth with a pair of tongs. Japanese restaurants—even McDonald's—almost always pass out moist cloths for washing your hands before you eat.

"Your spiciest soup," grumbled the alien safari hunter. "And make it a double helping."

"Big day ahead of you?"

"What business is that of yours?" he snarled.

"My profound apologies, good sir," she replied, bowing. "I will place your order immediately."

The alien grunted and brusquely turned his attention to a small black item he'd removed from a jacket pocket. It looked like a BlackBerry or some other smartphone, but I could see with a glance that it hadn't been manufactured by any Earth-based company.

I climbed to the brim of his hat and looked down, making a thorough study of the device—its shape, its color, and the specifications of the tiny screen, which, at least for the moment, simply read, AWAITING SIGNAL.

I zipped to the men's room, transformed myself back into human form, and returned to the counter. My plan was simple: I was going to get my hands on his tracking device, and I was going to do it without him knowing I'd done it.

"Can I take your order, young man?" asked Dana, passing me a washcloth.

"Yes, miss, I'd like a steaming hot bowl of *whackami,* please," I said to her with a wink, using the Alpar Nokian word for "distraction" in place of the Japanese word *wakame,* which means seaweed, and was one of the flavors of soup featured on the menu.

She winked back. "And would you like a large or small serving, sir?"

"Might as well make it a large," I said. "And if you could," I whispered, "please time it to arrive exactly when you bring lunch to that gentleman down the counter."

I pulled out my iPhone and pretended to read some manga while Dana went back to the kitchen. In a moment she returned with a very large—I'm talking bigger than her head—bowl of soup, and carried it down the counter.

I tensed, ready to spring to action.

"Here's your soup, sir," she said, placing the bowl of soup on the counter in front of the alien.

"Fine," he muttered without glancing it up. "Leave it there."

"Would you like some hot sauce?"

He looked up from the tracking device and glared. "I *said* I wanted it spicy — *of course* I want hot sauce."

"Very good, sir," said Dana, reaching under the counter and pulling out a bottle of shishito chili oil. "Will this do?"

He squinted down at the bottle's label and nodded. But, as he did, Dana squeezed the full bottle ever so slightly, causing a single droplet of the oil to spurt out and into the alien's left eye.

Shishito chilies are legendary for their potency, and after handling them Japanese cooks know very well not to touch their faces, particularly their eyes. The stinging and burning can be so intense that temporary blindness often results.

With a muffled yelp, the hunter dropped the tracking device onto the counter and jammed his washcloth into his eye, rubbing furiously and shouting all manner of alien curse words. If it hadn't been a brightly lit, crowded restaurant, I'm sure he would have leaped across the counter and throttled Dana without a moment's hesitation.

Instead, he snarled at her: "Would you . . . please . . . get me . . . a clean *washcloth!*"

I quickly transformed a stack of napkins into something that looked exactly like his tracking device. And then it was a simple matter of sidling up behind him and making the old switcheroo while Dana hurried to get him a clean cloth so he could dab his eye.

"You are a fool," he spat out as he ripped the towel from her hands.

"A thousand apologies, good sir," she said. "May I offer you a free cup of tea?"

"You can offer me nothing, you pathetic lower life-form," he grumbled. He was about to say something more hostile than that, but he stopped himself. Instead, he grabbed his newly replaced tracking device and stormed out of the restaurant.

"This is some excellent seaweed soup," I told Dana as she passed me the check.

"I thought you'd like it." She smiled as I shelled out the appropriate combination of yen notes and coins and scribbled some instructions on the back of the check for her to meet me outside.

Chapter 35

TEN MINUTES LATER I'd gotten us a fortieth-floor room in the Park Hyatt—the swankiest high-rise Western-style hotel in the area—and I summoned the rest of the gang.

With Joe's help, we quickly determined that there was more to the alien's smartphone than I'd begun to guess. Not only was it tuned to a secure channel that would receive transmissions from Number 7 and Number 8, but it contained a preloaded database about the nearly extinct Pleionid species and its abilities, as well as a smattering of other encrypted information that I hadn't been able to access from their heavily secured network.

Joe had run a signal from the device straight to the wide-screen unit on the wall, so we could all see the information it contained.

"They spoke in colors!" exclaimed Emma. "How amazing!"

The transponder was now displaying images from the Pleionid's home world—a cloud land of shifting colors and shapes, mesmerizing in their complexity and beauty. And there, flitting in and out among the semisolid shapes—their towns, their buildings?—were the Pleionids themselves. Sweet, wide-eyed creatures that seemed to be a cross between ET, a long-haired terrier, and maybe Alvin of Alvin and the Chipmunks.

But that form was apparently just a default. They easily, effortlessly, became balls of pulsing light, lightning streaks of pure color, and nearly transparent clouds that floated hither and thither. Sometimes, they even seemed to turn completely invisible.

The screen now filled with a chemical study of what I quickly realized must be pleiochromatech, the unique life-blood of these creatures that, combined with their pacifist ways, had led to their demise. I'd never seen anything so beautiful in its chemical complexity. It seriously put the DNA double helix to shame. Its structure—containing elements ranging from neon to lithium to magnesium—looped, intersected, folded, and refolded itself in front of our eyes. Impossibly, it seemed to be a *living* molecule.

Now the screen showed the Pleionid home world of today: a gray, dusty cinder of a planet. Just another burned-out orb, like so many others the Outer Ones had left in their wake.

Emma was practically sobbing at the sight, and the rest of us weren't far behind. Joe shut off the feed.

"Anything else, Joe?" I asked.

"They haven't activated the tracking program yet, but it should work once they release the activation code. And I think I've figured out how to triangulate any signal we get on the Pleionid—hopefully that will help us find it before the other hunters do."

"What about intelligence on the other safari hunters, or on Number 7 and Number 8?"

"Nothing really, but there's one image here..."

And right then, the screen lit up with a headshot of another alien. An all-too-familiar and disturbing one.

It was a high-res photo of *me*.

BOOK TWO

SEE YOU LATER, SPACE INVADER

Chapter 36

THE FACT THAT Number 7 and Number 8 had put my mug shot into the device meant, at a minimum, they wanted to warn the hunters of my presence in Tokyo. Quite possibly, it also meant I was the next target in their hunting "game."

I suffered through lectures, worried warnings, and a firestorm of pleadings from my friends to call the whole thing off. But either I acted now, or I let the universe's last living Pleionid die. So—after my friends were done saying every discouraging thing they had to say—I politely thanked them for their concern and waved them out of material existence.

Now that I had the hunter's tracking device and we had pored over every piece of its data that we could unlock, there was only one lead left to pursue in the hours before the hunt began—Kildare Gygax.

I'd learned he was going to participate in the Pleionid hunt. I also knew he was the child of my two immediate foes. But my most compelling interest in Number 7 and Number 8's kid had to do with an unshakable hunch that he wasn't as simpatico with his parents as they might have hoped. Besides, I knew something about feeling distant from your parents.

Of course, it still took quite a lot to psych myself up and go to his school to find him. Never mind the obvious risks, there was also the matter of that horrible, soul-scarring school uniform, the *seifuku*, I had to wear. I swear, even the ever-kind Emma would die laughing if she ever saw me in it. And Willy, Joe, and Dana—forget about it. They'd probably call me Sailor Boy until the day I died.

I choked down my last shred of dignity and put on the ridiculous thing.

Having spent the morning stealing and analyzing the hunt transponder, I didn't arrive at school until lunchtime break. Unlike most of the other kids, Kildare was not out on the playing fields; I found him alone in the science lab intently studying ants in a glass terrarium. With all my senses on high alert—ready to fight or take flight as the circumstances dictated—I approached and cleared my throat.

He whipped around so fast, I swear, even the ants in the terrarium jumped in surprise.

Chapter 37

"WHAT ARE YOU doing here, Daniel? Why weren't you in class this morning?"

"Um, you know, immigration stuff."

He looked me up and down, and, though I've seen more convinced expressions, he nodded. He had a notepad in front of him with formulas scribbled all over it.

"What are they doing?" I asked, bending down to look at the ants.

"Their favorite thing—eating," he said.

The ants were swarming over a lump of something white and were methodically carving it into transportable pieces that they carried back to the nest entrance one by one.

"What was it?" I asked.

"A turnip," he replied.

"Good thing turnips don't have nervous systems, huh?" I said. "That looks like it might hurt."

"Yes," said Kildare, looking up at me. "It's definitely a very lucky thing for turnips and anything else that ends up in front of a hungry colony of ants if it's unable to feel pain."

I nodded grimly, trying not to imagine what it might be like to be stung to death and then carved up into a few million bite-size pieces. "It's amazing how coordinated they are. How they work so well together."

"They use pheromones," Kildare explained. "They lay down scents and other chemical markers that affect each others' behavior. As social communications systems go, it's unrivaled. They can even stalk and kill prey thousands of times larger than themselves."

"Of course, *Myrmecina nipponica* don't do a whole lot of hunting, do they? Aren't they pretty common house ants here in Japan?"

He looked at me with surprise. "This terrarium isn't labeled. How did you know the name of this species?"

"Big Edward O. Wilson fan, dedicated Discovery Channel viewer, and budding entomologist, I guess," I improvised.

"Me, too." He smiled and turned back to the ants. "Actually, you're right about their dietary habits," he went on. "More than ninety-eight percent of what ants eat is vegetative or already dead. Some species can and do hunt other living animals, but their reputation as predators is grossly exaggerated."

"And that's a good thing," I said, "considering they represent more than fifteen percent of the biomass of all creatures on Earth—more than ten times that of all living humans—or they might eat us all up."

"Yes," he said, looking up at me again with a curious smile. "It's a very good thing."

Just then, the door opened and Professor Kuniyoshi came in with two students.

"Ah, Kildare," he said. "How's the colony?"

"Very healthy, Professor," replied Kildare. "I expect they'll soon be fledging."

"Good news, good news!" beamed the teacher, taking the two students to his desk to review some papers.

Kildare remained focused on the ants, perfectly content not to talk. I couldn't help liking him, but he was definitely an intense kid. There's an old Japanese saying—still waters run deep—and something told me I hadn't a clue what lay in the depths of Kildare's personality.

Chapter 38

IT FELT ROTTEN spying on Kildare, but I had no choice but to follow him when school got out. After all, I'd only known him for a day. It wasn't like I could ask him what he knew about his parents and the Pleionid hunt in the middle of class.

I expected him to go home to the GC Tower, but I wasn't completely surprised when he headed in the opposite direction instead. I trailed him down the street, onto a bus, to a Mister Donut—where he bought a dozen glazed—and then to the *shinkansen* station. He seemed distinctly gloomy, and I again wondered what he might be thinking about tonight's hunt. Was he really just going along with it for some almost-human reason, like maybe he wanted to please his father?

Not, of course, that it really mattered. Right then I had

more immediate things to figure out—like where the heck he was going. The bullet train he was boarding ran out to the northeast suburbs of Nishinasuno and beyond.

I'm pretty good at tailing people, if I do say so myself, but we'd only gone twenty minutes when he nearly gave me the slip. The train was hurtling through the fields outside of Kurodahara when I noticed him getting up from his seat and heading forward, maybe to use the bathroom in the next car.

But no sooner had he exited the car than I happened to spot him *out the window!*

Somehow he'd gotten himself off the train and was striding through a rice field like he was a farmer out for a stroll.

With a quick "Pardon me" to the middle-aged commuter at my side, I made my way to the bathroom, then teleported myself off the train, something that I assure you is much easier said than done. I didn't know the area very well, so, to be safe—and to make sure I didn't teleport myself into a rock or something—I simply rematerialized myself five feet off the ground and on the opposite side of the train, in case Kildare happened to look back in my direction. Only problem was I forgot to materialize at a speed relative to the ground. That meant I was still traveling as fast as the bullet train.

Yeah, over one hundred miles per hour. Ouch is right.

I bounced and rolled like one of those Olympic downhill skiers who wipes out halfway through the course, only my wipeout was in a muddy, flat field. It was a good thing

I'm a pretty sturdily built kid and that there weren't any trees. It was also a good thing Kildare was too far away to hear me crash to the ground.

Once I'd determined I wasn't mortally wounded, I turned myself into a butterfly whose anatomy I'd fortunately had occasion to memorize from Professor Kuniyoshi's collection. I caught up with Kildare just as he made his way to a moss-covered old Buddhist lantern at the edge of a small field.

The timing was good, because what happened there was something I really had to see with my own eyes. As Kildare approached the stone lantern and placed his hand on it, the moss began to move—*and talk!*

Chapter 39

THE PLEIONID!

The creature had been waiting for Kildare cleverly disguised as a layer of moss and lichen on the surface of the ancient lantern.

Despite its being maybe the cutest creature I'd ever seen—those big puppy eyes, those adorable little hands and feet—it tore into Kildare's bag of Mister Donut donuts with ravenous savagery. Then it collapsed to the ground in a fit of satisfied groans and bubbly giggles.

But Kildare wasn't smiling as I landed on a nearby stalk of bamboo.

"You can't stay here," said Kildare. "They're coming for you in less than an hour. You need to leave this planet. *Now.*"

"I need to talk to the boy," it replied.

The *boy*? Did it mean me?

"He was at my school today," replied Kildare.

My little butterfly mind was racing at a thousand miles an hour. Did Kildare know who I was? I guessed that would make sense given that his parents had mug shots of me floating around their information network.

"Take me to him," said the Pleionid.

"There's no time," Kildare told him. "And I don't think you can help him anyhow."

"Faith," the Pleionid responded simply.

"I have faith," said Kildare, glancing at his not-yet-activated hunting tracking unit. "I have faith their gamers will hunt you down, and then my parents will probably eat your carcass if you don't get very, very far away from here *right now*."

Should I have revealed myself then and there? It seemed an obvious thing to do. But was it *too* obvious? How was I supposed to be certain this wasn't a trap?

The answer, of course, was that I couldn't be certain of anything. I bit my butterfly tongue and stayed right there, looking to all the world just like one of its billions of innocuous insects.

Chapter 40

HOW MUCH TIME was I losing just resting there and debating everything I saw through my thousand-lensed butterfly eyes?

There was no way Kildare could be the enemy, I thought. I mean, what kind of evil space alien *practically bawls his eyes out* saying good-bye to a creature of an entirely different species, one that his parents want to kill and eat?

I could only imagine what my father would say if he knew I was forty miles outside Tokyo developing sympathies for the son of Number 7 and Number 8 on The List of Alien Outlaws on Terra Firma: I was just too darn gullible. When you think about it, wasn't that precisely why I'd failed to notice that the little girl in the test had really been an alien? I saw her, and, like some just-landed-on-Earth simpleton, I assumed she was a poor, sweet little innocent whose life it was my mission to save from demon motorcyclists. Now, here I was out in the real world stalking my *real* enemies, and yet this time I didn't think it could be a trap?

Still, the way the creature had simply replied, "Faith," to Kildare, kept echoing in my head. Why shouldn't I have faith in my own instincts? Hadn't I gotten this far relying on them?

The second I made up my mind to begin to turn back into my regular self, the creature raced up, belched a cloud of donut-scented gas in my face, and, with a distinct note of mischief, said, "Catch me if you can, *Alien Hunter!*"

Startled, I tumbled to the ground, the stalk of bamboo crushed by my sudden human weight.

"Wha—*Daniel?*" Kildare said, as shocked as I was. "How did you find us?"

I ignored him and kept my eyes on the Pleionid. "You said you wanted to find *me!*" I blurted as I struggled to my feet.

"If you are who I think you are, you won't have too much trouble," the Pleionid replied, winking a puppy eye at me and breaking into bubbly giggles again. "Can't be too cautious!"

And, with that, it was gone. Or, rather, it would have seemed gone if I hadn't been aware of some of its abilities and known what to look for. A nearly-impossible-to-detect flicker of motion, like the faintest breath of wind in the grass, was racing across the field.

"Where's it going?" I yelled back at Kildare, already sprinting after the Pleionid.

"You'll have to catch him to find out!" Kildare shouted, fading away behind me as I hit—thirty, forty, fifty, sixty, seventy, eighty miles per hour—trying desperately to catch up.

It was racing right for the train tracks, which, I quickly realized, were about to be occupied by a Tokyo-bound *shinkansen*, hurtling our way at more than a hundred miles per hour.

I put on an additional burst of speed, sending up a rooster-tail of mud and rice plants behind me. I felt a little bad—some farmer was going to be upset at the furrow I was making through his paddy—but there wasn't time to apologize or to fix things right then.

I was just a dozen or so yards behind the Pleionid when I realized it was aiming to cross the tracks a split second ahead of the approaching bullet train, thereby trapping me on the other side of it or, perhaps, leaving me smeared across its pointed nose.

Fortunately, I happen to be able to leap higher than a speeding locomotive. *Un*fortunately, as I cleared the hurtling train, I didn't see any sign of the Pleionid.

What I did see was an alien I recognized from the GC Tower boardroom.

A *hunter*.

145

Chapter 41

THE OWL-FACED GOON was squatting in the rice paddy and had some serious alien-tech camouflage going on. But since I was coming down from thirty feet in the air, it wasn't hard to see him or his wicked-looking weapons.

Of course, I was brilliantly disguised as a teenager taking a superhuman leap over a bullet train, so it wasn't too hard for him to see me either. His wicked-looking weapons were soon blasting away in my general direction.

I hit the ground and leaped sideways, then—faster than any bullet train—I charged. Getting in low under his spray of weapon fire, I tackled him, then I applied that *kansetsu waza* joint-locking move that Miyu had used on me. In a moment, I was standing on his armored neck and looking down into his panic-stricken, silver-eyed, noseless face.

"You're — you're —" he gasped.

"Yeah," I said, "your friendly neighborhood Alien Hunter. Now tell me, what are you doing here?"

"The Puh-puh-puh-plee —"

"Pleionid?" I asked.

He nodded and started sputtering again: "Puh-puh-puh-please don't hurt me. I'll leave Earth, I promise!"

"Tell me how you tracked it here. The hunt codes weren't supposed to go out till the hunt started, and that's not for another half hour."

"I ha-ha-ha — hacked the system."

"How does it work?"

"It tracks pleiochromatech emissions. N-n-n-now, will you puh-puh-please let me go?"

"Why would I do that?"

"So you can *die*, Alien Hunter!"

And, with that, I came to realize that owl-headed goons like that one have certain defense mechanisms I'd failed to anticipate. I won't give you the blow-by-blow on what happened next, because it gets a little gross, and your parents or teachers might take this book away from you if I spelled it out in too much detail. But let's just say this particular breed of alien — the Dookian — when under duress, is apt to spray the highly caustic contents of its intestines at its attacker.

The long and the short of it is that this one did it *to me*, and it was easily the single-most-disgusting experience of my life. Fortunately, however, it wasn't fatal and didn't prevent me from karate-chopping him into the next prefecture.

When I was done cleaning his repulsive goo off me — I had to materialize a full case and a half of Handi Wipes to get the job done — I found the tracking unit he'd hacked and quickly determined that the Pleionid had already gotten thirty miles ahead of me, heading east toward Narita Airport.

I took off running at a comfortable two hundred miles per hour (any faster and I usually get a bit of a headache from the concentration it takes not to trip). Soon, I was closing in on my quarry.

But it wasn't headed quite all the way to Narita Airport. Instead, it stopped in the middle of a beautiful garden in the town of Ushiku. But it wasn't the plantings that were the most noteworthy feature of the place. That distinction went to a bronze man who happened to be taller than Godzilla.

Chapter 42

DEPENDING ON THE movie, Godzilla is seldom depicted as much bigger than two hundred and fifty feet tall. The Amitabha Buddha statue at Ushiku is almost *four hundred feet tall*, and that's not counting the base he stands on.

To give you some perspective, that means that it's more than twice the height of the Statue of Liberty; it also has a place in the Guinness World Records. Yeah, it's *that* ginormous.

Also suffice it to say the Pleionid wasn't content to meet me someplace convenient like a snack bar, ticket booth, or even in the viewing room located in the chest of the statue. No, my ultracamouflage little quarry went straight to the top—crawling like the world's fastest and most purposeful oil slick up the exterior of the colossus, all the way to the head, where it proceeded to lodge itself in the statue's left ear. I watched and watched (and kept checking the hacked tracking device) until it appeared that the Pleionid had finally stopped running.

Now I just needed to figure out how to get up into the Buddha's left ear without making the local news and the Facebook pages of every camera-wielding tourist on the grounds. Which basically ruled out sprouting wings like Maximum Ride, leaping like Superman, scaling the statue like Spiderman, or laying the statue down on its side like the Hulk.

So I ended up doing the tourist thing and rode as high as the attendant-driven elevator would take me: up into the statue's slit-windowed chest. From there, it was only modestly difficult to duck behind a display and do my tried-and-true butterfly trick. I flitted under the door marked WORKERS ONLY and soon found myself inside the cavernous, girder-spanned interior of the statue.

The statue's ears were open to the outside, although chicken wire had been put across them to keep birds and bats from roosting inside. That didn't stop the Pleionid, though. Without breaking the screen, it had somehow crossed through. Another trick I'd love to figure out.

"*Danaus plexippus,*" it said simply.

"What the—?" I said, with my typical articulateness.

"Your species of butterfly, Alien Hunter," it replied, its voice disarmingly rich and wise-sounding. "But why don't you turn yourself back into your human form. Your insect voice is hard for me to discern with the wind blowing up here."

Oh, yeah. I forgot I was a butterfly. I turned myself back

into my human form and looked down at the big-eyed, furry-skinned creature.

"Sorry for all the running," it said.

"No big deal," I replied, although I realized as I collapsed to the cool bronze floor that I was pretty darn sore from that little chase. "I'm thinking of taking up cross-country in the fall."

"Cross-country?"

"Running for school. It's a sport. You run outside."

"Ah, well," it said. "Now I have a sense for your 'cross-country' abilities. That was one reason why I had you chase me. To make sure that you were indeed the Alien Hunter. But also I needed to teach you something."

"Teach me?"

"Yes, Alien Hunter, teach you. My time is short. And we must ensure that yours is not."

"But you're safe for now. Why can't we just get you away from here, someplace where they can't find you?"

"As should be quite obvious from the fact that I am the very last, we Pleionids don't live forever. Now, give me your hand."

I laid my hand in its hand, thinking this couldn't possibly be a trap—and it wasn't. But what happened next was the last possible thing I would have expected.

My mind was bathed in color, light, shapes, motions, incredible beauty, unbearable sadness, and—most of all—an amazing depth of *understanding* I'd never experienced before.

Suddenly, I saw how Pleionids had harnessed the

chemistry of pleiochromatech to change shape, to make themselves practically invisible, to squeeze through tiny crevices, to radiate color, to share thoughts *by touch*. Most stunning of all, it gave me a glimpse of the true beauty of our universe—and of the horror of the threats that face it.

In short, it gave me the biggest mojo download of my whole life.

"Wh-wha—"

"Don't say a word," it urged, smiling up at me faintly and pulling its hand away. "I have to go now. And this time, don't follow, okay?"

My mind was still wading through a newfound sea of light and knowledge, and all I could do was nod and stutter my thanks.

"Don't forget the good, Daniel," the Pleionid said. "And now, if you would, please *duck!*"

Chapter 43

I REFLEXIVELY DROPPED to my belly as an enormous inky black shape brushed past me. *What the heck?* I sprang to my feet just in time to see the black form widen. It happened too quickly to get a good look, but the creature seemed to resemble one of those bizarre-looking, huge-mouthed, predatory deep-sea fish—except that it could fly. It opened its enormous, long-toothed jaws, aiming for the Pleionid.

"No!" I shouted, diving into its path. In less than a second, I had turned myself into a stick of the hardest substance I could think of: diamond. And I was now wedged between the open jaws of the inky black shape. It shook its head and roared in frustration, and I felt my stick-shaped self start to tremble. Diamonds may be one of the hardest substances on Earth, but this guy was definitely from another planet.

"Thank you, Alien Hunter," the Pleionid said sadly. "But it is now my time. You must not sacrifice yourself. The world needs you."

"No! Don't do it!" I screamed. But the Pleionid was already leaping toward me. He knocked me out from between the alien's jaws, which came crashing down and *swallowed the Pleionid whole.*

I will carry that image to my grave.

A wave of nausea came over me as the Pleionid's killer somehow passed out of the statue's ear and into the night. But there wasn't time to react—more shapes were coming up behind me, and fast!

I was sure that as a diamond I'd end up in one of these goons' pockets, so I changed myself back to human form and spun around. Climbing up the girders toward me were a half dozen of the hunters I'd seen in Number 7 and Number 8's boardroom meeting.

"Double bonus," hooted one of them.

"The Alien Hunter and the Pleionid on the same safari!" another yelled. "We'll be famous!"

"Don't let him out!" shouted one of the taller hunters as he did one of those two-finger Special Operations gestures where you tell your squadmates to fan out.

Wait a minute. They were supposed to be solo agents. So why were they working *together*? I could hear them racking and priming their weapons and in a moment the whole place stunk of ozone and molten metal as a half dozen plasma pulses arced through the darkness toward me.

Still reeling from the horrific vision of the black shadow

of death swallowing that beatific little creature, I somehow managed to leap over their heads, grab a lateral girder, and pivot myself down through the darkness to the interior roof of the viewing room, a few stories below. I can only imagine what the tourists inside thought when hearing all the thumps, weapon pulses, and shouting over their heads.

And then there was an awful whine, a whine I knew from dreams as well as I did from real life—one of those conscienceless alien poachers was priming an *Opus 24/24!*

Great. This was just great. Human civilians under my feet, a sacred metal statue all around me, a half dozen aliens working together to blow my brains out, and I was so tired and disoriented and scared I could barely see straight. Some superhero I was turning out to be. If the cards continued to fall like this, I would be responsible for the untimely deaths of more than a hundred innocent souls.

Then in a flash, I realized the Opus 24/24 was no longer charging, which meant it would soon be *firing*.

I leaped up as a pulse of pure pain arced from a saw-toothed muzzle, and evil yellow tendrils blossomed across the interior metalwork of the statue.

Normally I would have stood my ground, normally I would have been happy to go down swinging, but normally I wasn't living with the burden of just having witnessed the death of the last member of a legendary—and irreplaceable—alien species. I couldn't even think straight. Heck, I probably would have had trouble tying my shoelaces right then, I was so freaked out.

And then it came to me—pleiochromatech. I'd just been shown how to make it and how it worked. I didn't need to fight; I could *hide*.

I dove down into the wealth of knowledge the Pleoinid had just given me...and through an act of sheer will that I don't know how to explain, I flattened myself into a slick of invisible flesh, and slid down into the darkness while my pursuers raged with frustration.

Chapter 44

THEY SAY THE best way to recover from a tragedy is to throw yourself back into regular life. And since the only regular thing I know to do in this life is hunt bad aliens, that's exactly what I did.

At 8:20 a.m. I was on my way back to school to have one last meeting with Kildare. I couldn't shake my hunch that he was part of the solution, not the problem. And the alternative—waving the white flag and leaving Japan like my father wanted me to—just wasn't in the cards. Especially not after I'd learned that Number 7 and Number 8 weren't a couple steps away from having the human race destroy itself; they were *one* step away. And not after I'd just let the last living Pleionid get eaten by some nameless, faceless, game-obsessed alien beast.

As it turned out, though, I didn't have to get all the way

back to school to find Kildare. Three blocks away from the main entrance, I just about collided with him as he rounded a corner on his bicycle.

"Hey," I said as he skidded to a stop. His eyes were red and puffy.

"Oh, Daniel, hey."

"Want to give me a lift the rest of the way?" I asked. "I could sit on the rack."

"I'm not going to school," he blurted. "My father won't let me go anymore."

"Your dad is actually *forbidding* you to go to school? What is he—like, the *Anti*-Dad?"

He started to say something but clamped his mouth shut before it could get out. The pain in his eyes said it all.

"Well, small world," I quipped, trying to cheer him up. "I'm having a crapalicious day, too."

He nodded and tried to smile, but the poor guy was starting to shake.

"Hey," I said, "I know just the thing."

"You're going to go make my father change his mind?"

"Better than that. You and I are going to take one of the most important courses of study that school offers."

"But I told you, my dad's not letting me go."

"This is an off-campus course."

He looked at me skeptically. "Oh yeah? What's it called?"

"Introduction to . . . *hooky*."

Chapter 45

WE HEADED STRAIGHT to Harajuku, the hippest district in the entire city of Tokyo. From Burton Snowboards to Harley-Davidson to Under Armour to North Face to Adidas—name your favorite company and they have a store in Harajuku. And, chances are, it's mobbed with teenagers.

Oh, and it's also got some pretty hip cafés, clubs, and fancy Japanese restaurants. But I wasn't in the mood for noodles or sushi for lunch, so, instead, we hit a Shakey's Pizza, where I can't recommend the dessert pizza enough. That's right—a pizza crust with such toppings as pineapple chunks, hot fudge sauce, and whipped cream.

"I feel a little sick," said Kildare with only a mild smile of regret. After eating an entire teriyaki chicken pizza, he'd somehow managed to down an entire 1800 cc Grande

Parfait (read: a half gallon of ice cream floating in a syrupy maelstrom of flavored toppings), and apparently his alien digestive system wasn't any more robust than mine. We went outside and attempted to recover from our respective food overdoses on a pedestrian overpass, looking down at the sea of people coursing up and down the sidewalks like ants at an overstocked picnic.

"I guess they must call this the Shakey's shakes," Kildare joked weakly, looking down at his rumbling belly.

"Let's walk it off," I said, hoping the taste of pineapple and maraschino cherries would one day fade from my mouth. "Isn't Ueno Park right up the street?"

Ueno Park is an old-style city park—cobblestone carriage paths, huge trees, stone parapets—in the center of Tokyo. It's got more than a half dozen world-class museums in and around it, a zoo, playing fields, and some truly awe-inspiring Buddhist shrines.

We soon discovered that it's also got to be Japan's premiere cherry-blossom-viewing venue. There have to be more than a thousand cherry trees in the park. I mean, I'm not a huge flower freak or anything, but all those millions of blossoms—and how the petals rained down like a snowstorm when the wind blew—it's just one of those things you have to see to believe.

What was *not* so cool to see, however, was that on that particular spring afternoon, for every one of the thousands of blossoms on each of the trees, there had to be at least one tourist crammed into the park.

Plus, one alien safari hunter.

And believe me, one was enough. As luck would have it, it was the tall one whose hat I'd ridden on in the GC Tower elevator and whose tracking device I'd stolen. He was attempting to blend in as a forty-something man who happened to stand six feet eight inches tall and looked like he had broken glass under his skin.

We were just walking past the life-size model of a blue whale in front of the natural history museum when I spotted him. I grabbed Kildare's arm. I didn't need to offer a word of explanation as I steered him quickly away from the crowds toward the safety of a nearby shrine that had been roped off for the blossom festival.

As is customary, we washed our hands in the ablution pool outside the shrine.

"Should we stop the charade, Daniel?" he whispered as he filled his ladle with the cold water streaming from a spigot in the mouth of an ornately cast copper dragon.

"Of course, Kildare," I said.

"You aren't here to kill me; I can tell that much."

"That's true—and I'm sorry we haven't talked openly before. I just, well—"

"It's my fault too. Things are just so messed up. My parents—"

I nodded. It was definitely a delicate situation. Which was of course why we hadn't talked about it, even though obviously we'd both known each others' true identities all along.

"I hope it's okay. I feel bad—"

"They killed the Pleionid already, didn't they?"

I nodded.

"I felt it."

"Look," I said. "Is there anything you can tell me that will, um—"

"I know they have to be stopped, Daniel. But just give me a day. I think I may know a way to do it without resorting to, you know—"

"Okay. But what are you thinking?"

"I can sabotage my parents' plans."

"You mean like when you set the Murkami family free?" I asked, giving voice to a hunch.

He nodded.

"Steps like that aren't enough, Kildare. They have too much in motion now for us to be doing guerrilla stuff. They're too strong. We have to step it up. How many others will they hunt to extinction?"

"Well," said Kildare. "I'll give you one thing you may find useful if, you know, my plan doesn't work."

"Please. Anything."

He nodded as he ladled some more water over his hands. "Do you like the ocean?"

"What?"

"Oh, crap!"

He was staring across the pool. I followed his horror-stricken gaze and saw Ellie and Colin Gygax—his parents, Number 7 and Number 8 on The List of Alien Outlaws on Terra Firma—coming up the stone path toward us. They did not look happy.

Chapter 46

"DANIEL, THEY'RE GOING to try to demoralize you. Don't let them, okay? No matter what they say."

"I don't demoralize easily," I replied. Still, I had to admit I was more than a little freaked out that they somehow knew we were here and were approaching us in broad daylight!

"Good," Kildare said. "Now just stick with me."

My mind was exploding with questions, but I nodded at him as his parents came up to us, looking like some snooty, well-dressed professional couple.

"We can do this right here, right now, in the middle of Tokyo, Alien Hunter," said Number 7, striding up and attempting to grab Kildare's hand. Kildare was having none of it and backed up next to me.

163

"Of course, given the crowds today, a few hundred humans would doubtless be killed or injured in the melee," chimed in Number 8. "Minimum."

"Like that's a big concern for you guys," I muttered.

They ignored me, and Number 7 went on. "And we'd doubtless end up wrecking some of this park's lovely cultural treasures—"

"We mean, *if* you still want to *hunt* us, that is."

"You're calling *him* a hunter?" demanded Kildare.

"Why else would he have been conducting surveillance on us?"

"Shopping in our store—"

"Watching us from window-washing platforms—"

"Turning himself into a fly—"

My mind was reeling. How did they know all this? How had they been spying on me even as I was trying to spy on them?

"Even," said Number 8, "going as far as pretending to care about our son."

"He *does* care about me," protested Kildare. "Way more than either of you do."

"*Sure* he does, son," said Number 7. "That must be why they call him the *Alien Hunter.*"

"It's not very nice pretending to be somebody's friend like that," said Number 8, casting a reproachful glance my way. "But what would you expect from an Alpar Nokian?"

"Yes, cold-blooded killers, all of them. He was just using you so he could find out more about us—so he could more easily hunt our family," said Number 7.

"Yes, isn't that one of the first things they teach you as an Alien Hunter — to *know your prey?*"

"At least his version of hunting involves saving lives; not killing for *sport*," Kildare shouted.

"So he wants to *kill* us to *save* lives?" replied Number 7. "Perhaps he should consider taking a course in logic?"

"Or," continued Number 8, "perhaps now that he knows more about us, he should just throw in the towel?"

"Yes, perhaps," said Number 7, "he's beginning to realize we're a bit more trouble than we're worth."

"Unless," continued Number 8, suddenly turning to me, "you need some more convincing?"

"Like," said Number 7, "maybe it would help you to know that we're not who we appear to be?"

"That we're colonial beings," said Number 8, "composed of billions of intelligent particles —"

"Which can combine," continued Number 7 as he took his wife's hand, "and take on any shape we wish —"

His voice suddenly sounded not so much like a single voice but a whole crowd of people talking at once. And then the two of them suddenly flickered gray and began to merge, effectively doubling in size and taking on a massive cloudlike swarm. It was kind of like somebody had just kicked over the world's biggest hornet nest, and the hornets were on steroids and under the control of an evil supergenius. The cloud descended on a nearby pine tree and, with a stomach-turning buzzing noise, consumed every single branch and needle, leaving behind a burnt-looking stump.

At the top of the shrine's stairs, out of earshot but still within view of us, the attending monk let out a small yelp and fled into the park.

Number 7 and Number 8 morphed back into their usual separate forms as I tried to lift my jaw from the ground and not look quite as surprised as I was. The implications of their being colonial creatures were past alarming to consider. Shape-shifting, immunity to projectiles, immunity to blunt trauma, able to disperse and reassemble at any time—

"So, tell us, have you ever fought a cloud that can take any form it wants and has a collective intelligence higher than any army the universe has ever known?" asked Number 7.

"It has its challenges, we assure you," said Number 8.

They didn't need to tell me. What was I going to do? Drop a bomb on them in the middle of a Tokyo park?

"Yes, why don't you be a smart little Alien Hunter and leave us alone?"

"He's *not* going to leave you alone," yelled Kildare. "And I'm going to help him!"

"But surely not right now—not in this crowded park, not where so many innocents might be hurt?"

I nodded at them coolly.

Just then Number 7's cell phone began to ring, and he pulled it out of his pocket.

"Is it him?" asked Number 8.

"It is," said Number 7 looking down at the readout of his smartphone.

"We'll continue this later," said Number 8 as Number 7 put the phone to his ear. And, just like that, the two of them turned and walked back down the path, out of the now quiet sanctuary and into the crowded, blossom-filled park.

Chapter 47

"CAN YOU DO that?" I asked Kildare as we hurried to the train station. Number 7 and Number 8 were gone, but something told me we weren't exactly being left alone. My plan was to return to the Fujiya Hotel and then summon my friends and family to meet Kildare.

"Am I a colony too? Is that what you're asking?"

"I saw you turn gray like that once, at school. When Ichi stuck you in the garbage can."

"We call it 'dispersing' if you want to know the technical term. Yeah, I'm *really* their son. But personality's a different thing, you know. Just because you have a brain like your parents' doesn't mean you're going to think the same thoughts or believe the same things."

"I wasn't saying—" I started.

"I know. And I don't mean to be defensive. It's just that

my parents are a little harder to relate to than those of most kids. I mean, some kids complain about having moms and dads that are lawyers or insurance agents. They should try coming home to a couple of vicious genocidal maniacs—"

"—with a small army of henchmen," I added, gesturing at two aliens shambling down the path toward us in too-tight warm-up suits. We might have mistaken them for sumo wrestlers, except that, once again, their knees bent the wrong way.

"Yeah," he agreed as we broke into a run toward the Ueno Station on the JR Yamanote line. But even as we made it down the park steps to the sidewalk, we spied three more badly dressed alien henchmen waiting beneath the overpass just outside the station. One of them waved while the other two reached inside their hoodies and pulled out weapons like the ones I had seen in the box back at the Game Consortium.

This was *not* good.

"Taxi!" I yelled, stepping out to the curb and flagging down a boxy little Tokyo cab. It's no easier finding an empty cab in Tokyo than it is in New York, Paris, or London, but one just happened to be there right then.

We quickly hopped into the backseat. "Omiya, please," I said, identifying a major train station a good distance out of downtown where we could easily find a train.

"Anywhere you like, bosss," hissed the driver.

"Oh, crap!" said Kildare with alarm. "It's one of my parents' Silurians!"

Silurians are a species of monkey-like reptile frequently hired as contract assassins, because they're clever, patient, and obedient, and happen to enjoy killing so much that you don't even need to pay them to do it.

The driver quickly locked the doors and hit a button that started blowing knockout gas through the vents. Fortunately, Kildare hadn't quite closed his door and we leaped back out to the sidewalk as the cab accelerated away.

"Close one," gasped Kildare.

"We could have taken him," I said, "I *think*."

"Well, something tells me my parents have a few more agents in reserve."

"I think you're right. And I also think, judging by how they had the JR station covered and now this cab, that they're expecting us to try to get out of town."

"So?"

"So, we're doing exactly what they expect us to do, which must mean we're making things easy on them."

"So we should do the opposite of what they're expecting, like—"

My mind raced as I spotted two more alien thugs making their way toward us down the crowded sidewalk.

"Let's not go out of town; let's go *down*town."

"Downtown where?"

"Know anyplace to play video games?"

Chapter 48

IT WAS A fairly long walk, but at least it proved to be one free from alien harassment.

"Looks like they really weren't expecting us to go this way," I remarked as we crossed the pedestrian bridge over a rail yard a few blocks from the looming GC Tower.

"That," said Kildare, "or they *wanted* us to do this and decided to make it easy."

"Thanks," I told him. "For a minute there I'd actually forgotten to feel paranoid."

"I can't remember the last time I didn't feel paranoid," Kildare said, gesturing at a bench. "Is it okay if we rest here?"

I nodded as he took a seat. I was about to sit down myself when I caught a whiff of something so delicious I couldn't think straight.

"What *is* that?" I asked Kildare, inhaling deeply.

"Krispy Kreme," Kildare's voice caught, and he nodded somberly at the far end of the overpass where I spotted a Krispy Kreme donut shop sign.

I looked at his furrowed brow. "Um," I said, trying not to drown in my own saliva, but realizing something was troubling my friend. "What's up?"

"Nothing. They used to be his favorite."

"Krispy Kremes? Whose?"

"The Pleionid. After school he used to disguise himself and ride in on my backpack. We'd stand in line and then we'd buy like three dozen glazed and sneak off to an alley and scarf them down together."

"You miss him, huh?"

"You know what it's like to lose somebody close to totally senseless violence, don't you, Daniel?"

I nodded. "Why did your parents do it, Kildare? Why did they kill the Pleionid? Why do they hunt creatures to extinction?"

Kildare shook his head. "I wish I knew. They weren't always like this. I wouldn't go so far as to say they were ever kind to me, but at least they used to look after me. Lately, it's like I'm just another alien employee."

"What happened?"

"I don't know, but it doesn't matter now, does it? They're murderers. Mass murderers."

"But they're your parents," I said. "So you want to give them one last chance. I get it. Do you want to fill me in on your plan? Maybe I can help."

"You're helping already. You're giving me hope, Daniel." He got up from the bench. "Now let's go get some donuts, and then we can head over to the GC Tower."

"No need for the donuts," said a familiar voice behind us.

Number 7 was standing there holding an open box of Krispy Kremes.

Chapter 49

WHAT CHOICE DID we have? Out of deference to Kildare's plan—if not to the thousands of innocent humans around us in crowded downtown Tokyo—we fell into step with Kildare's father and let him lead us the remaining three blocks to the GC Tower.

Number 8 and a ghoulishly grinning gaggle of security guards met us on the sidewalk and escorted us through the mob of frustrated teenage boys who had gathered outside the flagship store, which was, the sign said, CLOSED FOR A PRIVATE EVENT.

"We're so glad you decided to join us," said Number 8 as two guards unlocked the doors and escorted us into the lobby. "We've been wanting to beta test some new games, and you two are smack in the middle of our target demographic."

"Yes," said Number 7, "for instance, we have a new 3-D simulator called Teenage Geek Squad, in which two unpopular boys get caught up in circumstances far beyond their control."

"Yes," said Number 8. "And we want you to try out another new title called NTAC, which stands for 'No-Talent Alien Clowns.' You get to play two delusional characters who think they're going to save the world but who inevitably end up getting their butts kicked all over the place."

"And after that," said Number 7, "we have a prototype for a high-concept strategy game along the lines of World of Warcraft but involving competing groups of aliens who've invaded a planet populated by a species of complete losers and mean to make the most of its abundant resources."

"Or, if you'd like," said Number 8, "we have another title based on a superhero-comic concept called Alien Hunter: The Dim Knave. It's about a kid who goes out thinking he has amazing superpowers only to gradually realize they're all in his head and that while he thinks he's been fighting evil, he's really only been fighting progress. And he has a laugh-riot sidekick, a kid so delusional he thinks that his own parents are his worst enemies."

"Sounds hilarious," said Kildare, deadpan.

"It *is*," said Number 7. "Although, if you start to feel overstimulated, we can try some off-line games too. Things like this—"

And, with that, steel shutters dropped across the store windows, and the two security guards pulled out their sidearms and began blasting away. At me.

Chapter 50

"MOM, DAD! DON'T!" screamed Kildare. "He's not going to hurt you!"

If this was all part of Kildare's plan, he sure was a good actor. I leaped over a console of driving simulators and tried to find some cover, which wasn't easy since their weapons were making short work of the video-game consoles. If they kept this up, their entire store would soon be reduced to a circuit-board scrap heap.

I know I'd told Kildare I'd give him a day before I went after his parents; but I didn't recall making a similar pledge about their security goons. I grabbed the turret-mounted gun off the first-person-shooter console next to me and quickly transformed the thing's guts into those of an Embulsorator 2300—a weapon my father favored and whose popular nickname was the Fly Daddy, so called because it turned your opponent into a harmless species of insect.

I leaped back over a bank of consoles with my seemingly plastic gun. No doubt assuming it was a harmless video-game accessory, the security goons promptly burst into laughter.

"Anybody know how to turn this thing on?" I asked, taking advantage of their overconfident amusement and gradually leveling the gun at them. They laughed even harder until I depressed the trigger, and, voilà, their suddenly not-smiling selves turned into tiny little flies that—unlike when I turned myself into an insect—didn't include their brains. They were, for *all* intents and purposes, plain-old flies forevermore.

"He's harmless, is he, Kildare?" asked Number 7. A sharp smell was wafting through the room. I immediately realized it was the same odor I'd detected in the crawl spaces upstairs in the Tower when I'd found Kildare's secret room.

"He won't hurt you," repeated Kildare, with little spirit. My friend had become very pale and was shaking. He looked like he was getting sick, but not with the common cold.

"I promised him I wouldn't harm you," I told his parents. "Now let us out of here."

"Won't hurt us, huh?" asked Number 7. "The great Alien Hunter is taking an early retirement?"

"Or," suggested Number 8, "perhaps the reason you're not going to harm us is that you've discovered you couldn't if you tried?"

"At any rate," said Number 7, "the relevant fact here is that *we* haven't made any such promises about not harming *you*."

And, with that, he shot out his arms and sprayed a stream of white liquid at me, which I'm glad I didn't assume to be nondairy creamer. I did a backward flip and landed ten yards away as the liquid hit the tile floor and melted through to the level below us.

Next time I had a chance, I guess I'd have to add that to their entry on the List computer: can shoot ultraconcentrated acid.

Now Number 8 had joined the action, easily mimicking my flip—despite the fact that she was wearing a woman's business suit and heels—and landing right next to me. I smiled sheepishly as she looked down at my surprised expression.

"My home world has stronger gravity than yours," she explained. And then her arms turned gray and became wicked-sharp-looking swords that she swung together toward my neck like a giant pair of scissors.

I ducked and sprang to Kildare's side in the middle of the showroom floor.

"You okay?" I asked. Number 7 was looking at Kildare intently, and for some weird reason his cheeks were puffed out and he was *blowing*.

"He's . . . making . . . pheromo—"

"Pheromones!" I blurted. Of course! That was the sharp odor I'd been smelling. And that must be why Kildare looked so sick. If the "cells" of his body and his parents'

bodies worked the same way those of the ants in his terrarium did, Number 7 was disrupting the very function of
Kildare's bodily systems.

"Here you go," I said, materializing a gas mask and
quickly putting it over Kildare's face.

He nodded and put his hand on my shoulder as he
breathed deeply through the mask. Already he was straightening back up, and color was returning to his skin. But we
couldn't exactly savor the moment because Ellie Scissor-
Arms was sprinting toward us, her razor arms whistling
through the air as she came. And if that wasn't bad enough,
Number 7 had produced a shoulder-firing microwave can-
non from someplace and was in the process of drawing a
bead on us. Before I could grab Kildare and drag him to
safety, he pulled off his mask and did one of the most
amazing things I've ever seen.

He pulled in his feet and hands and for a moment hovered there off the floor in a curled-up ball. Then Kildare
flickered gray and—BLAM!—exploded into a dim gray
cloud that entirely filled the room.

A new sharp smell assaulted my nostrils and stung my
eyes, then both his parents flickered gray and dispersed
into indistinct gray clouds.

The demolished store was now filled with an angry
buzzing sound, and Kildare rematerialized.

"It won't last too long," he said. "And I won't be able to
surprise them that easily again," he said.

"Another pheromone?"

"Yeah, panic signal," he said. "I'd never tried it before,

but I just set off an alarm that sends all their cells scrambling. Kind of like when you stir up a hornet's nest or an ant hill."

We bolted out into the lobby. The steel security shutters had now dropped around the perimeter of the building, and there was no obvious way out. I sized up one of the shutters and got ready to magnify my strength and peel it from its frame.

"So that panic signal you used on them is kind of a self-preservation thing?" I asked, stooping down to grab the shutter.

"Exactly," said a voice behind me. But it wasn't Kildare's.

Chapter 51

THE VOICE DIDN'T belong to Number 7 or Number 8, either; it belonged to *both* of them. Kildare's trick had scattered them into their billions of parts, but they had now regathered. Well, sort of. Together they'd formed a dense, swirling gray cloud, with four black eyes and a single cavernous mouth the corners of which rose in a bone-chilling smile as I turned around.

"Yesss," *they* hissed to me. "We have many talents that single-body creatures like you can't begin to guess."

Kildare was standing frozen next to me. He'd gone completely white except for his widened eyes, which were now completely black like those of his parents.

"Kildare?!" I yelled at him, but he didn't react. It was like his mind had slipped away, and then, to my horror, *his body started to disappear too.*

He was being swallowed. Number 7 and Number 8's mouth had grown to the size of a whale's, and their body was expanding like a bellows, drawing in air—and drawing in their son. He came apart like a pillar of sand in a tornado. They were devouring him!

It was so terrifying an image that my emotions were getting in the way of my powers. My head was reeling, and I couldn't figure out a thing to do about it. How was I supposed to hurt a cloud? And how was I supposed to defeat the enemy and *not* hurt Kildare?

"That's right, Alien Hunter. Another of our unique defense mechanisms involves eating our young. At least the ones that are weak or unfit."

"Give him back," I commanded. "He's not like you."

"You're right—he's not *like* us. He's *part* of us."

"Give him back," I repeated, this time with as much authority and ire as I could muster. But they sensed my weakness here. Had it all been a trap? Did they somehow lead me to Kildare, to lure me back to them? Had he intentionally fooled me?

"Here's the deal, Alien Hunter," they announced vaingloriously. "You have thirty seconds, and it's your choice how you spend them. If it's any comfort, we can assure you that you'll soon get to see Kildare—or, at least, *parts* of him."

Rage boiled up inside me, but I couldn't just blindly attack them. I didn't want to hurt my friend. I had to play along. "What do you mean by that?"

"You can either stay here and chat with us, as you're doing now," they continued, "or you can have a head start."

"A head start? What are we playing, tag?"

"You can call it whatever you like, but we tend to refer to it as 'hunting.' And then once we've caught you, we'll devour you, just as we did Kildare. Only in your case, it will be a lot more painful and *permanent*."

"Oh, look at that," taunted the black-eyed cloud, morphing part of itself into a wrist with a watch wrapped around it, at which it glanced dramatically. "Time's up!"

My ears filled with an awful buzzing sound as the cloud began to envelop me.

BOOK THREE

LONG DAY'S JOURNEY INTO NIGHT

Chapter 52

EVER GET STUNG by a bee or a yellow jacket or a fire ant? Try all three at once, and then multiply the feeling by a thousand if you want some sense of the intense pain I experienced when Number 7 and Number 8 first grazed my left arm. If a doctor had shown up and offered to amputate my afflicted limb, I would have said yes on the spot.

But almost worse than the pain was the frustration. I couldn't figure out how to fight back. It was a textbook case: often the greatest challenge of my powers isn't actually using them; it's deciding *how* to use them. And while I believe there are elegant solutions to every problem under the sun, finding the right one usually takes more than a few seconds, or minutes, or hours, or…

I dodged another dark blow from my amorphous

four-eyed enemy as I gave up on the latest of several half-baked ideas, including:

- Sucking them up with a giant vacuum cleaner. Problem was, did I really expect they'd stay sealed in the bag and I could just toss them into a Dumpster?
- Using a flamethrower might be effective, but I'd run the risk of burning Kildare's cells too, assuming he was somehow still alive in there...
- Preserving them cryogenically with a freeze ray and then spending the next few years figuring out how to extract Kildare's billions of cells from the mix once they weren't moving around. Problem was that although I'd heard of them, I hadn't yet learned the physics of freeze rays and couldn't very easily just invent one on the spot.
- Using a giant can of alien bug spray was a great idea, *if* I had any understanding of Number 7 and Number 8's physiology and what toxins might actually be effective. And, again, how could I simultaneously *not* kill the Kildare parts of the cloud?
- Going back in time and hoping things would work out differently. But I'd been told that Number 1 had somehow put a block on time travel for me, and since I had no idea how he'd done it, I couldn't possibly figure out how to work around it.
- Summoning a billion carnivorous dragonflies and instructing them to eat only those bits that looked like Number 7 and Number 8's cells. I had no idea, though, if there actually were a way to tell Kildare's

bits apart from his parents' bits...or if a billion dragonflies would fit inside the lobby...or if dragonflies
were even trainable.

In short, maybe if I'd had a month and access to the
intergalactic equivalent of Wikipedia, I could have come
up with something. But I didn't have a month. And I didn't
have a computer. And I *did* have a big black cloud of malev-
olent alien cells trying to sting me to death.

Again and again, they came after me. At first I was dodging pretty well—biding some time, hoping against hope I'd
find a weakness, a chink in their amorphous armor—but
with every leap, spin, duck, and parry, I grew a little less
confident, and a little slower, and a little more scared.

And then blackness exploded across my vision, and
searing white light seemed to be pouring into my skull.

They'd hit me. They'd gotten me in the face.

How could I have been so stupid? How could I have let
them do this to me? How could I have thought—after losing Kildare, after my friends' and father's warnings—that
I'd ever stand a chance against them?

I leaped blindly, as high and as fast as I could, wanting
only to get away, wanting only to make the pain stop.

I smashed into the wall on the far side of the room with
a bone-jarring thud, but I was almost grateful for it. The
stinging wasn't as bad as before, and my vision had partially come back. Apparently, they'd only grazed me.

And then, finally—as if the impact had knocked some
sense into me—I had a halfway decent idea.

Chapter 53

I'D NOTICED THAT every time Number 7 and Number 8's cloud attacked me, it first had oriented its four eyes at me. Its *eyes!* In other words, it was finding me by *sight*. If the cloud *couldn't* find me by sight, I might just gain some sort of advantage or, at least, a chance to live.

The next step was effortless. I filled the entire GC Tower lobby with something relatively easy to understand and create: mirrored glass. With a quick sweep of my arms, I converted the sleek obsidian ground floor of the building into a giant carnival fun house.

The fun part was that Number 7 and Number 8 didn't see just me; they saw *thousands* of me.

The not-so-fun part was that, judging from the angry, droning roar that went up, they weren't very happy about it.

"You think you're *clever?!*" the cloud's polyphonic voice

challenged me, spinning its gray mass around and around as it—or they?—tried to figure which image was the real Daniel X.

This was no time for chitchat. I had to take advantage of their momentary confusion to strike back or get away.

The cloud's eyes were up against one of the mirrors now, examining the surface closely, very closely. Then it lifted a glossy black appendage—an arm? a leg? a tentacle? a pseudopod?—and carefully tapped the glass.

There was a small *ping* and then the pane shattered into gravel-sized bits and collapsed on the hard floor.

"*Not* so clever," the droning voices yelled triumphantly. The cloud flickered and launched a swarm of tiny, glossy black spheres. In a moment, they had all fanned out and had shattered every single mirror in the room, resulting in a sound like, well, a Niagara-sized waterfall of breaking glass.

All of them, that is, except for the one that was obstinately flying into my forehead, over and over again, wondering why on earth I wouldn't shatter.

I grabbed it in my fist, and it made a disgusting popping sound as I crushed the life out of it.

"Ouch," pouted the cloud's voices as it turned its four baleful black eyes toward me.

"You started it," I reminded them, as a wall of darkness roared near. I almost got out of the way, but it hit me in the leg—hard.

And then I began to fall, and my entire being exploded in pain, and, well, I don't remember much after that...

Chapter 54

I DIDN'T WANT to open my eyes. They hurt enough as it was with the lids closed, without having to focus or move or do anything. I just wanted to go back to sleep. I just wanted to fade back into darkness. I just wanted get myself away from the sickening, searing pain that racked my head and entire body.

"Daniel, sit up. You need to drink."

The noise hurt my head, but there was something reassuring about the voice, something that was the closest thing to comfort I could remember.

And then I realized why. It was Dana's voice.

"Am I dead?" I managed to croak, no pun intended.

"Almost—but you somehow teleported yourself away before they could actually kill you."

"I don't remember trying to teleport," I said with a wince. "I was in too much pain."

"Maybe it was the pain that forced you to do it," Dana said. "You couldn't stand it any longer and channeled all your energy into getting away. There's no shame in backing down when you know you need to. It's what we've all been trying to tell you from the beginning."

I decided I would have to think about that some more later. "Where are we? Are we safe?"

"You're back at the Amitabha Buddha in Ushiku."

"The giant one?"

"Yes, the one that could kick King Kong's butt."

"You mean if the statue were alive and King Kong were real?"

"Yes, Daniel, that's exactly what I mean."

I cautiously let one of my swollen eyes open. It was dark.

"Is it nighttime?"

"Yes, you've been unconscious awhile."

"Wow, it's *really* dark," I said, allowing my other eye to open. "Even for nighttime."

"Well, that's because we're inside the statue's head. There aren't a lot of light sources in here."

"So . . . why are we inside a Buddha statue's head?"

"Because that's where you teleported yourself, genius."

"I teleported myself? Away from Number 7 and Number 8?"

"That's what I was just telling you. Don't you remember anything?"

"Would I be asking—" I couldn't finish the sentence. I had to stop talking. My brain was wobbling like bowl of jelly on a dirt bike's fender. Dana forced a Japanese lemon soda to my lips. It was really sour, but it felt good in my sore, dry mouth. I drained the entire bottle in less than five seconds, a new personal best.

"That's it. Drink up. Clearly, you aren't ready to heal yourself yet," said Dana, taking the soda and resting my head gently in her lap. "So, get some sleep. Let your body do some of the work on its own. I'll be right here."

It's true—between the pain and the exhaustion, there was no way I could possibly think about doing something as complicated as diagnosing and fixing my wounds. You know why doctors have to go to school for like ten years before they get licensed? It's because healing is a complicated business. Way too complicated for somebody as beaten down as I was then. But I wasn't going to stress about it. After all, Dana was right there next to me. Seemed like nothing bad ever happened when Dana was around. I turned my head and started to thank her, but she pressed her finger to my lips.

"Shhh. You should sleep, Daniel."

I did want to sleep. But I also wanted to figure things out. I wanted to figure out if Number 7 and Number 8 had done any permanent damage to my body or mind. I wanted to figure out what Dana might be thinking right now. I wanted to figure out what that weird high-pitched droning sound was.

"Is that my stomach, Dana?"

"I wish," she said, jumping to her feet and letting my

poor aching head slam down on the steel platform where we'd been resting.

"Ow!" I complained. "I'm injured here."

"You'll think you were just tickled by a feather if we don't get out of here right now. That noise is coming from an alien skycar. *The hunters are coming!*"

Chapter 55

AS YOU MAY recall, I'm quite capable of running at over two hundred miles per hour. Limping at that rate of speed, however, is an entirely different sport and not one I'd recommend.

At that velocity, the forces that come into play are pretty extreme. But when your leg has recently been mauled by a couple of top-ten List aliens and feels like it was broken in three places and then sprayed with hot acid...

In other words, I wasn't really too keen on the idea of going all the way back to Tokyo on foot. We ran as far as a highway overpass and stopped to look back at the alien vehicle now hovering above the giant Buddha's head like an oversized mosquito.

I zoomed in my eyes and turned up the light levels, watching closely as the vehicle slowly circled the head.

I gathered it was running some sort of scan to determine whether I was in there or not.

"Uh-oh," said Dana, with good reason. The skycar had changed direction and was now pointed right at us. And it was accelerating toward us at one hundred, two hundred, three hundred miles per hour! I'd have trouble running that fast on a good day. Trying to materialize our own skycar now, or even a motorcycle, just wasn't possible.

"Daniel, you *teleported*. That's how you escaped Number 7 and Number 8 and ended up in the Buddha's head. You've got to be able to do at least that much again."

I could almost see the driver's eyes through the windshield of the rocketing skycar.

"Gotcha," I mumbled. I just needed to think of a place to send us. A place whose layout I knew, a place that would be the same as when I was last there, a place where a person—or a piece of furniture—wouldn't be in our landing spot, inadvertently causing us to be dead on arrival.

And I needed to figure it out fast, before we got mowed down by the approaching alien vehicle that was now a mere one hundred...fifty...twenty-five...ten yards away.

Chapter 56

THE WEIRDEST THING about teleporting is how instantaneous it is. There are no flickering lights or humming sounds like on *Star Trek*. One eyeblink, you're looking at one thing, and the next, you're looking at something else. It's even faster than changing TV channels and definitely faster than waiting for a website to load. It's just slam bam, okay, here I am.

"The dojo!" exclaimed Dana as we looked around the abandoned Keihin martial arts studio where we'd sparred with our friends the Murkamis.

"Yeah," I said, "I thought it fitting to go back to the first of the many places I've had my butt kicked in Tokyo. Nostalgia thing, you know."

"Stop feeling sorry for yourself, and start figuring out

how those aliens knew to find you, or we'll never get a moment's rest."

I looked out the dojo window and saw the orange lights of the Tokyo Tower looming over the city skyline. An image of the schematics Number 7 had been looking at flashed in my head.

"I'm honestly not sure how they always seem to know where I am," I said. "But I'm pretty sure I know how they're letting the hunters know about it."

"How?"

"Let's go do some sightseeing," I answered instead, nodding at the Tower's blinking lights.

"Are you okay to go out? You still look terrible, Daniel."

"You were the one just saying that we can't sit still. They'll come after us again unless we do something about it."

Dana frowned. "Hey! What's happening to your leg?"

I looked down at the more battered of my legs—the one that felt like it had been broken in three places—and saw that it was changing shape.

And I don't mean that it was just swelling up a little. I'm talking *morphing out*.

My leg was literally sprouting rainbow-colored fur and flexing and stretching and shrinking and then becoming invisible. And before I had a chance to freak out about *that,* it started rematerializing (without the rainbow fur) and stretching and shrinking and then popping back into its usual shape.

At the same time, a feeling of cool relief washed over me. The leg was no longer giving me any pain. It actually felt darn good.

"Daniel, what the heck was that?"

For a moment I was unsure myself. I hadn't *consciously* healed myself. Then a bubbly giggle echoed in my head.

"I think I must have picked up a little something from the Pleionid," I said to Dana.

"It taught you how to heal yourself? Why didn't you do it earlier?"

"Because I didn't do it. It kind of did it by itself."

"Weird. But your leg's better?"

"Right as rain," I said.

"Prove it," she said.

"Sure!" I grinned, nodding at the Tower. "Wanna race?"

The leg was better. I even set a new personal best. Four hundred thirty-eight miles per hour! My sneakers were a little worse for wear, but that's okay. Unlike colonial alien supervillains, I *understand* sneakers. So I made myself a fresh pair.

Chapter 57

AFTER WHIPPING OUT the tracking device I'd stolen and doing a little triangulation, I confirmed my hunch about how Number 7 and Number 8 were directing the hunters to find me: the aliens had installed a relay transmitter in the top of the Tokyo Tower, something I'd figured out from the schematics I'd seen on Number 7's computer.

It stood to reason: the Tokyo Tower was one of the tallest structures around, and if you wanted your signal to have the widest possible range, you wanted your source as high above the ground as possible.

Fortunately, getting up to the top of the tower wasn't a problem. The tourist center was closed, there were no crowds, and it was pretty dark. So I simply took advantage of my much-improved leg and climbed up the outside on the structural girders. Dana was right behind me, whistling the theme from *Spiderman* as we went.

The transmitter was alien-tech and, therefore, a very compact package. Since it broadcast an ultralow frequency and in an incredibly sophisticated pattern, humans would probably never detect it in a thousand years. What *was* more noticeable, however, were the sticky, black, rubbery balls—slightly bigger than watermelons—that were clustered at the base of the tower's broadcast mast.

"Gross," Dana remarked.

"Definitely not native to Earth," I observed, taking some readings on my modified iPhone. "But they appear to be completely inert. They're probably leftover lunch containers or something."

I turned my attention to the small transmission device and proceeded to scan its length. In theory, there should have been a dataport I could use to reprogram or shut the thing down without setting off any alarms.

"Are you sure that's the right decision, Daniel?" asked Dana.

"What?"

"Ignoring those things."

"I found it! The dataport!" I said, attaching my tracking unit and ignoring her.

"Um, Daniel—"

"What?" I asked.

She didn't answer, but I heard weird cracking noises, then looked up from the display. Dana was silently backing up toward me.

Beyond her, the sticky black things were no longer sticky black things. They'd disgorged a half dozen metal-skinned creatures that were busy unfurling wings, fangs, claws, stingers, and a host of other appendages that you might expect if you were to cross a twenty-five-pound hornet with a sack of scissors.

"Oh," I said.

Chapter 58

FORTUNATELY, THE WINGED alien sentries (which, I assumed, Number 7 and Number 8 must have planted here to guard the transmitter) weren't quite ready to get airborne. Like any insect just emerging from its pupal stage, they had to extend their wings to dry before they could fly.

Nevertheless, they weren't exactly less than agile in moving each of their six feet. They came skittering forward, claws, fangs, stingers, and other shiny metal bits poised to poke some serious holes in the two of us.

"Daniel," Dana said in a steely voice.

"Yeah, I'm listening to you this time," I whispered nervously as I took in all of the clicking joints and clanking spikes. They moved terrifyingly *fast*, but in a mesmerizing sort of way.

"How about you forget your antigun bias this time and just materialize us some deadly weapons?"

She didn't have to say another word. In a few seconds we were holding two of Dad's favorite Fly Daddy transformers.

"Fire!" I commanded, and we let loose a stream of blasts from the weapons.

But the creatures—with reflexes the likes of which I'd seldom seen—turned away so that their metal-hardened upper carapaces reflected the fire harmlessly up into the air. Then, like turkey-sized bionic scorpions, they sprinted the remaining distance toward us.

Stunned, we both leaped to the next platform up the tower's mast.

"Holy moly, are they fast," I said, stating the obvious.

"Holy moly, are they *creepy*," Dana echoed.

We were on the second-highest platform in the tower's tip and in another moment had hopped up to the very highest level. Glittering, nighttime Tokyo was sprawled about us like some vast, twinkling circuit board. The view was spectacular, but there wasn't a moment to appreciate it.

I looked down the mast to gauge how much time we had until our attackers reached us, but just then the light at the top of the tower blinked on. My vision became a sea of eye-clenching red, and my ears filled with the thrum of the discharging capacitors that powered the light.

"Bright enough for ya?" asked Dana, rubbing her eyes as the lights went back out.

"They're to warn low-flying aircraft," I explained. "They have to be bright. Which also means they have to use a lot of electricity."

As the capacitors recharged, I examined the electrical conduits running into the lights and did some quick calculations.

"Okay," I announced. "On the count of three, we jump up again."

Dana pointed at the sky above us. "Don't know if you noticed, but... there are no more platforms to jump to."

"Just do it, 'kay? Straight up and as high as you can go."

She shrugged as I tried to tune out the ringing metallic sounds of our pursuers, concentrating instead on the increasingly higher pitch of the charging capacitors.

"One, two, three," I counted. *"Jump!"*

As soon as I'd delivered a swift kick to the conduit, Dana and I leaped up into the air. The high-tension wires spilled free and exposed the copper leads to the tower's structural steel.

I was only a couple feet in the air when the coordinated pulse emerged from the capacitors. It tore a new path swiftly through the tower's girders, then up the legs and through the bodies of the giant alien insects.

"Nice!" yelled Dana as we landed back on the platform and eyed the sizzling corpses of the guard bugs. Then I quickly repaired the wiring so we wouldn't get shocked ourselves and so that low-flying aircraft wouldn't have any trouble seeing the tower.

We scrambled back down to Number 7 and Number 8's

transmitter. "All set?" asked Dana, as I unplugged my handset from the device.

"All set. I just entered some new coordinates."

"New coordinates?"

"The transmitter—and the hunters—will now think I reside on a rocky island just south of the Comoros Islands off the coast of Africa."

"But won't that be dangerous for the people who live there?"

"It's uninhabited," I reassured her. "With any luck, the aliens will get frustrated and start hunting each other. Now, let's get moving."

Chapter 59

DID YOU EVER have a friend who you worried was doing something stupid, but you didn't want to be a busybody, so you stayed quiet and kept your opinion to yourself?

Looking through the glass at Kildare's ant colony in the science lab, I was realizing I'd just had a situation like that. I couldn't keep the what-ifs from running through my head. What if I'd argued with Kildare? What if I'd persuaded him not to pursue his plan? What if we'd regrouped and come up with a bold strategy that hadn't involved meekly going along with Number 7 to the GC flagship store? What if I'd just gone solo against his parents so that he didn't have to be involved? Why had I even gotten their poor son sucked into this mess?

I sighed and looked down at Kildare's ants. Maybe they were hungry. After all, they probably hadn't been fed since the other day. I materialized some food—a nice fresh turnip—and was removing the lid from the tank when I noticed they'd been digging a hole in the sand. At the bottom something white was poking through. A piece of paper!

I put the turnip in the corner of the tank and removed the paper. It was the page I'd seen Kildare scribbling on the last time we'd been in the lab.

I pored over the organic chemistry formulas he'd written down, all involving some high-energy, self-propelling reaction, resulting in a bunch of compounds I didn't recognize. In fact, the only things that made any sense to me were two heavily circled abbreviations in the center of the page: NaCl and H_2O, shorthand for sodium chloride—common table salt—and dihydrogen oxide, more commonly known as water.

Water and salt? I had some serious chemistry studies ahead of me, but now, thanks to Kildare, at least I knew where to go.

Chapter 60

NO BETTER PLACE to find salt and water than in the ocean, right? I headed out to the beach at Shirahama, a not-too-touristy surfer beach south of Tokyo on the mighty Pacific. It was a cool day, and only a handful of surfers were out trying their luck in the rolling surf, including the legendary Japanese wave rider Katsu. I looked on jealously, but I had homework to do.

Instead of a wetsuit and board, I materialized a beach umbrella, chair, and a three-foot-high stack of chemistry textbooks. I needed to identify and understand the nature of all the chemicals and the reactions that Kildare had written down for me.

The first thing I figured out was why organic chemistry is used as a weed-out course in so many advanced science degrees: it's a subject so difficult that to make it through you have to be really smart and really dedicated. Something told me if I hadn't been up against what I was right then, I would have been weeded out myself.

Still, I was making some progress—that is, when I wasn't busy dwelling on scary and depressing thoughts, like:

- How my father had told me from the beginning to give up and leave Japan because I wasn't ready to face this challenge.
- How Number 7 and Number 8 could take on any shape they wanted because they were composed of billions of intelligent parts.
- How my best nonimagined friend in the whole world had just been consumed by his parents.
- How my enemies had apparently been aware of my every move thus far.
- How these greedy, cannibalistic murderers were about to turn all the video-game addicts of the world into raging machines of destruction...
- And how I had *no idea* why all the surfers had just left the water and were now racing up the beach, screaming their heads off in sheer terror.

Chapter 61

I'D ALWAYS ENJOYED Godzilla movies, but I'd never found them to be particularly scary. Watching a guy in a rubber lizard suit step on model-train sets just isn't the sort of thing that gives me goose bumps. But looking out at the ocean right then, I wondered if perhaps that puzzling lack of fear of an enormous, fire-breathing, radioactive dinosaur didn't stem from a certain lack of imagination on my part.

Having suddenly experienced something like it first-hand, I can tell you it's incredibly disconcerting to witness the ocean boiling over like an overfilled pot of pasta as a forty-story crested reptile strides up into the shallows.

The creature's footsteps shook the ground so violently that the sand on the beach seemed to liquefy. The few trees toppled, and the dunes behind me undulated.

I didn't for a second think this was the real Godzilla. (Well, okay, maybe I did for *half* a second.) But when I noticed the creature had four black, lifeless eyes, I knew Number 7 and Number 8 were proving their boast that they could indeed take on *any* form they wished.

Kildare's formulas raced through my mind. Would I be able to put my crash course in chemistry to good use? Certainly the principal reagent—salt water—was available in sufficient quantities. There was just one question to answer: had I done enough cramming to pass the final exam?

Chapter 62

THE CREATURE'S FOOTSTEPS were registering on seismographs as far away as Beijing. As I rushed toward the water, I was forced to leap repeatedly into the air to avoid getting swallowed up in sandy fissures or washed a mile inland by a monster-induced tsunami.

It was no big surprise that getting *closer* to the creature wouldn't make things any safer. I needed to be at the water's edge, which meant being within range of its radioactive fire, its enormous feet, and its spiky, sixty-foot-long tail.

"Poor little Alien Hunter," it boomed, looking down at with me with a toothy display that might have been a sneer or a smile. "Not as high up on the food chain as you thought, are you?"

"Last time I checked, Alpar Nokians were still way

above monsters made out of nothing but brainless *bugs*," I shouted back, dodging a swipe from its enormous hand.

The Godzilla form roared and suddenly sprouted another head. Two of the black eyes moved into it. Then the heads turned to each other and began talking in booming monster voices.

"What a horrible little boy, Colin."

"The product of poor parenting, if you ask me, Ellie."

"Yeah," I yelled up at them, "my folks couldn't hold a candle to you two. I mean, not everybody thinks to raise their child on a diet of insults, neglect, and, of course, that fundamental pillar of good child rearing: *eating* your young."

"Oh, it's not just *our* young we eat," boomed Number 7's monster head.

"No, no," continued Number 8's head. "We eat *any* young."

"Or, truth be told," said Number 7, running a big forked tongue along his six-foot-high teeth, "even the not-so-young."

I could probably have come up with a good retort right then but my mind was elsewhere. Our little conversation had given me the chance I needed to apply some of my recent studies to Kildare's formulas. I'd begun by visualizing a series of molecules, then I measured the proper proportions, oriented a series of catalysts, and, finally, isolated the very precise conditions required to initiate the reaction.

And now it was time to stop visualizing and begin *creating*. I materialized a handful of the two principal reactants in Kildare's formula—one came out as a yellow powder, the other a greenish liquid—and quickly cast them down into the wave that just then was breaking at my feet.

What happened next wasn't magic; it was pure, hard-core science. But the results were so dramatic that I imagine the world's greatest magicians would have paid to see it themselves.

A scream like a billion wailing mice went up, and the two-headed Godzilla in front of me began to sway back and forth. Its screams became louder as it lunged for me, but instead of a giant hand swiping at me, there was nothing there.

Because the creature's body was melting away. Dissolving into tiny black globs of decomposing alien, which were now beginning to rain down on the beach.

"Get him! GET HIM!" the voices screeched, but its body was breaking down too quickly. "We are indestructible! This is IMPOSSIBLE!"

I jumped back as the now limbless torso began pitching forward and landed in a heap at my feet. I held my ground and watched as the entire beach became covered in a black slick of alien protoplasm.

You see, salt water plus 1.9 pounds of the compound created by Kildare's formulas result in a self-sustaining reaction that produces a gas which basically interrupts the communications between all the "cells" in the bodies of Number 7 and Number 8's species.

In other words, I'd created a kind of nerve gas that destroyed the bonds between the tiny pieces of Number 7 and Number 8. They literally fell apart in front of my eyes.

"That's for Kildare, you scum," I shouted.

But I felt no joy from having destroyed my nemeses. Instead, as I wiped the oily stuff from my eyes and ran out into the polluted water, all I felt was loss and horror at what I'd done. I dove again and again into the waves—flailing around, searching frantically.

This was not part of the plan. After all, it was *his* formula I'd followed. Kildare was supposed to be here.

Kildare was supposed to live.

Chapter 63

EXHAUSTED AND EYES stinging from tears, salt water, and alien goo, I crawled back up the beach and buried my face in the crook of my arm. In the distance, I heard the approaching *thump-thump-thump* of a helicopter. I should have gotten up and left the scene. No sense in me trying to explain to the Japanese coast guard what had happened. The surfers could handle that.

I thought I'd seen something in the chemical reaction, a way Kildare could have fortified his own cells to be resistant. But he'd clearly succumbed right along with his parents. There was no sign of him anywhere. He either hadn't had time, or he hadn't been willing, to save himself.

The thought of Kildare's loss being a noble sacrifice was too bitter a consolation to swallow. Of course, Number 7 and Number 8 had to be stopped. But how much hope and potential—and how good a friend—had I just destroyed?

I'd never felt so weary and uncertain as I did right then. What was the point of ridding the world of bad aliens if it meant I was killing the good guys, too?

"Gross, huh?"

I recognized the reedy voice immediately.

"Kildare!"

"Sorry about that—" he said as I leaped to my feet and rubbed my teary eyes. "Took me a minute to recoalesce."

What I did next I know I probably shouldn't have, but I couldn't help it: I grabbed him in the best bear hug I could manage. And he hugged me back.

"Kildare—"

"I know, Daniel," he said. We let go and awkwardly stepped away from each other. "You did it. I can't thank you enough."

"I couldn't have done it without you," I said. "What you did was so brave—"

He shook his head. "It had to be done. Just like now you have to take out Number 1."

"I've been thinking, Kildare. With your smarts and your abilities, what would you say about *joining* me? With your help, we could finish off the rest of the aliens on the List. I'll introduce you to Dana, Willy, Joe, Emma, my parents, Pork Chop.... You could be part of our group. My family."

He was smiling sadly and shaking his head. "I can't."

"What do you mean, you can't? You need to finish school or something?" I laughed.

"I resisted the reaction, but I . . . I can't go on."

"What? You're here. You're *alive*. Your parents aren't coming back."

"I'm too young to go on by myself, Daniel. My parents were still feeding me. It's how we develop. Until we achieve full maturity, we can't subsist on our own. We need mature colonies to sustain us."

"But there must be others besides your parents—"

"The irony is that even though my parents hunted other species to extinction, we were the last three of our kind."

"But on your home planet, surely—"

"My parents consumed them all. We were the last."

"But you came up with that formula. There must be something we can do with your chemistry and my powers that would work . . ."

He shook his head. "Keep up the good work, Daniel. And please say good-bye to Professor Kuniyoshi for me. He was a good teacher."

"Kildare, this can't be happening—"

But it was too late. He was already starting to flicker in and out. "Kildare! You're the only true friend I have—the only one who knows what it's like to be alone. Tell me what to do!"

"You know what to do, Daniel," he said, starting to slump. "Finish what you started. Save this planet. You're the Alien Hunter. And remember—you were my only true friend too."

Then he collapsed into a black slick at my feet.

I don't know how long I cried—my heart was breaking.

I hadn't lost someone I cared about in ages, and all the grief came flooding back fast and furious.

But Kildare was right. I was the Alien Hunter. I had a job to do. A big one. I had to pull myself together.

After a few deep breaths, I grabbed a handful of the blackened sand, stuck it into my pocket, and ran up to the dunes above the beach.

EPILOGUE

EPILOGUE

Chapter 64

BACK AT THE Fujiya Hotel, the gang—Mom, Dad, Pork Chop, Dana, Emma, Willy, Joe, and the Murkamis—did their best to comfort me, and they did manage to lift my spirits a degree or two. I attribute most of it to watching Joe chow down on the eleven-course meal he'd ordered from room service. Let's just say it's a good thing I didn't have trouble diverting funds from GC's corporate holdings into my credit card account, or I'd have been faced with doing a couple years' worth of dishes when the room bill came due.

My family had put up holograms of my friends and Alpar Nokian relatives, including my grandmother, Blaleen; Chordata the elephant; Uncle Kraffleprog; and my cousin Lylah. But, unlike the Gathering Day party, the mood was respectfully subdued.

Dana was the first one to take me aside. She led me out to the balcony.

"Promise me Number 1's not out there this time," I said.

"I can't speak for your imagination, but we just did a sweep of the hotel grounds. It's safe."

It was a beautiful day up in the mountains. The cherry trees were still blooming, and the breeze carried the scent of the proud cedars that dominated the craggy terrain.

"You going to be okay, Daniel?" asked Dana, sliding the door closed behind us.

I nodded and rubbed my eyes with the back of my hand, vainly hoping to forestall tears.

"It's tough losing friends, isn't it?"

I nodded again and sucked in a big lungful of cool mountain air.

"You're too young to have been through so much," she said, taking my hand.

"Yeah," I agreed, still blotting my eyes and trying to smile. "Definitely stops being character building after a while."

"You have so much strength, Daniel. Nothing will ever stop the pain of a loss like that, but you *will* keep getting stronger. And you *will* keep saving lives—good lives of good people, like Kildare. You know that, don't you?"

I shrugged.

"Remember, we're still just teenagers. We have most of our lives ahead of us. And that's a lot."

The door slid open behind me, and Dana let go of my hand.

"Come on inside, you two," said Mom. "The Murkamis are leaving, and we need to say good-bye."

Chapter 65

THEY SAY AFTER a great tragedy, the only thing to do...

I woke up in the middle of the night and pulled out my List computer. I went right to the top—to Number 1's entry: The Prayer.

Oh, how I was going to take him down. Oh, how I was going to make him pay for everything he'd done to me. I was done losing friends. I was done losing family. I was done waking up in the middle of the night worrying about my life and the lives of the people and creatures I loved.

They said I wasn't ready for Number 7 and Number 8, and they were wrong. I'd taken them both out at once. And now I was going to show that evil space bug just how strong he'd made me. I was going to cut the head off his precious List, and I was going to live like a normal person.

A normal person with a regular life, with regular concerns, and with no more pits in my stomach about not having avenged the lives of my parents and my friends.

Something touched my shoulder, and I wheeled around, dropping the computer to the floor and instantly creating an Opus 24/24.

"It's okay, Daniel. It's me."

Dad.

"You've come a long, long way, Daniel. And I was wrong to doubt you were ready for Number 7 and Number 8."

"Glad you're able to let go of that one, sensei," I said bitterly, still primed for a fight, I guess.

He winced but nodded. "I had that coming," he admitted. "But please don't entirely discount my advice from now on. I was wrong, but my concern wasn't unwarranted."

I wrinkled my mouth and nodded. "What did you want to tell me?"

"I want to tell you not to go after Number 1 — not yet."

"Why doesn't this surprise me?"

"No question, you've suffered a lot, Daniel. And now to have lost Kildare..."

"Yeah!" I blurted, stung even by the mention of my dead friend's name. "I'm getting much more experience losing than I am hunting. Maybe they should call me the Alien Loser instead, huh?"

Dad shook his head. "Let me ask just one thing of you, Daniel."

"Sure," I said. I knew I was being a jerk. I softened my

voice and looked him in the eye for the first time. "Name it, Dad."

"You know what it's like to lose a best friend. Promise me you'll at least try to understand what it would be like to lose...a son."

Read on for a sneak preview of the new Daniel X novel

DANIEL X: ARMAGEDDON

Coming October 2012

One

I HAVE NEVER felt so alone in a crowd.

I was penned in, crushed by a horde of seriously evil thugs who, fortunately, didn't realize I had infiltrated their ranks. I surged with the teeming mob down a stifling corridor carved through a solid mass of black anthracite. Coal dust filled the air. And my lungs.

I did not belong here. Not in a million years.

Which might explain why I was so petrified.

Like the sea of murky shadows bobbing all around me, I was cloaked in a black robe with a pointed black hoodie—a cape I had quickly materialized so I could tag along with this legion of alien outlaw freaks.

Trust me: I *needed* to blend in.

If just one of these fiendish outlanders discovered I was Daniel X, it'd be time to open the orange marmalade.

I'd be toast.

Burnt, *black* toast.

After all, I am the Alien Hunter, legendary destroyer of

1

the universe's most evil extraterrestrials—including some of these goons' first and second cousins.

Disguised, and with my face hidden under my cloak, I moved with the murmuring rabble from the mineshaft into a foul and fiery chamber. The cavernous room looked like a dark cathedral. Jagged stalactites jutted out of the ceiling fifty feet up and oozed droplets of molten lava. Slick cave walls glistened with the light of a million flickering torch flames. A suffocating scent of sulfur tinged the acrid air.

Now I wasn't just petrified. I was also feeling kind of queasy. Sulfur, with its rotten-egg odor, has never been my favorite non-metal on the Periodic Table of Elements.

"Where are you from?" I heard a nearby alien grunt, luckily not to me.

"San Francisco. You?"

"Phnom Penh."

"Nairobi," snarled another.

These guys were definitely out-of-towners—from *way* out of town. Alien creatures from far-off galaxies. Extraterrestrial terrorists who lived, disguised as humans, all over the globe. And each and every one of these mutant monsters had come to this secret subterranean conclave to learn the same thing I had snuck down here to find out: Where on Earth were they preparing to strike next?

Suddenly a wall of fire shot up from an elevated stone platform at the center of the underground arena. A wave of cheers roared through the gathering as a gaseous fireball exploded and *Number 2 himself* stepped through the swirling whirlpool of smoke and flame.

That's right. Number 2. *Numero Dos*. The second-most-heinous villain on The List of Alien Outlaws currently residing on Earth.

I could tell instantly that this fiend had earned his second-seed ranking the hard way. All seven of my senses informed me that I was in the presence of pure, undiluted, high-octane evil. He looked the part, too. The demon astride the elevated stage towered over all the other beastly creatures. Enormous wings jutted out of his bony back. Red-hot rage seared his sunken eye sockets.

After momentarily savoring the adulation of his fawning fans, Number 2 raised both of his muscle-rippled arms to silence the crowd.

"My disciples! My cohorts! I have waited many centuries for this moment, this ultimate battle. Now, at last, my time has come! The final reckoning is at hand!"

The mob roared, stomped its feet, and shot up various tentacles and slimy appendages. Number 2 had his minions mesmerized.

All except this one stooge — Number 30-something on The List. I couldn't remember the gutbucket with the googly eyes' precise rank because, well, I tend to concentrate on the seriously twisted alpha dogs in the Top Ten, not the one-hit wonders down below.

Unfortunately, Mr. 30-whatever *was* concentrating his googly eyes on me.

3

In fact, he was staring straight at me, licking his slick amphibian lips and drooling.

"You!" he growled as he puffed out his enormous blow-frog chin and chest. I could tell: the toady bootlicker not only recognized me, he was all set to score some serious brownie points by ratting me out to his fearsome leader.

Too bad I never gave him that chance.

Señor 30-something had given me a pretty terrific idea by proudly puffing himself up like that. Since I was born with the awesome ability to rearrange matter at will—yeah, you copy that?—I quickly morphed the bulging blowhard into a hot-air balloon. Buffeted by thermals roiling up from the steamy horde below, the slick black blimp shot up toward the ceiling and all those pointy-tipped stalactites. He was definitely on his way to bursting his own bubble.

But he never made it that high.

The conventioneer from California whipped out his Bolide Blaster and, in a masterful display of indoor skeet shooting, torched the zeppelin in midair, initiating an awesome indoor fireworks display. The late Mr. 30-something exploded into a spectacular shower of fire flowers, glowing embers, and glittering streaks.

Raucous laughter, led by Number 2, echoed off the cavern walls.

My cover had not been blown, but the same could not be said for Mr. 30-something.

His cover—not to mention everything else—had been blown to bits.

Two

"PREPARE FOR ARMAGEDDON," hissed Number 2, his words dripping black-hearted viciousness. "It is time for the total annihilation!"

All around me, alien outlaw freaks were foaming at the mouth. Literally.

This was it, the moment they'd all been waiting for.

The one *I'd* been dreading.

"Attacks on Washington, New York, London, Paris, Moscow, and Beijing will soon commence. Los Angeles, Frankfurt, Rome, Chicago, and Tokyo will also tremble and fall. I will crush their small towns and villages: Ames, Iowa, and Marietta, Georgia. Edam in the Netherlands and Malacca in Malaysia. Not a single earthling will be spared as I lay waste to their so-called civilization."

As you can probably tell, Number 2 and his hench-lackeys had a pretty low opinion of humanity. Then again, I'm pretty sure none of them had ever bothered checking out Michelangelo's *David*, a Beethoven symphony, or an orange-and-white swirl cone down on the Jersey shore.

"This planet is ripe for the taking," the demon continued, his voice cold, confident, and eerily intelligent. "The human race has never been more divided, more short-sighted, more consumed with greed, or more inflamed by religious differences. Before I am through, all of humanity will hail me as their new Lord and Master. They will gladly embrace all that I believe in and become my slaves."

The crowd growled its approval.

Number 2 silenced them with a simple, savage flick of the wrist. "There is, however, one who has the power to stop all I seek to accomplish. A young boy. A teenager."

A few of his henchbeasts dared to laugh, until Number 2 glared at them with his red-hot laser-pointer eyes. Suddenly sizzling red beams shot out of the leader's eyes and threw the laughing monsters halfway across the cavern, where they remained motionless on the ground.

"If you fear me—and you should—then fear this child! He has already destroyed many of the universe's most powerful warriors. Never underestimate his abilities because of his youth." He gestured at the gargantuan cloud of gray smoke billowing up behind him. "Never underestimate Daniel X!"

Right on cue, my mug shot flashed into view on that thirty-foot-tall smoke screen. I was squinting, had a zit near my nose, and basically looked like a total scrungrow. They must've found the yearbook from the one school where I actually hung around long enough for picture day.

"Find him," said Number 2, his voice weirdly serene. "Bring Daniel to me and, rest assured, I *will* destroy him."

Needless to say, destroying Number 2 was high on *my* to-do list, too. But I had to wonder: Was there really any conceivable way for me, a teenager, to stop him, a lethally powerful alien commanding an army of murderous minions?

And what did this say about Number 1? If Number 2 could command a force this enormous, how huge was Number 1's army?

"You will receive further instructions in due course," said Number 2 as his wings creaked open. "For the present, your mission is quite simple: Find the boy. Bring him to me."

All around me, grotesque alien beings sprouted webbed wings and collapsed into themselves as if they were gray, gauzy umbrellas. I quickly realized what was going on: Number 2's storm troopers were turning themselves into *Diphylla ecaudata*.

Vampire bats.

In an instant, I was surrounded by thousands upon thousands of unbelievably ugly, bloodsucking, wing-flapping, furry fiends—all of them shrieking with glee.

Well, you know what they say: When in hell, do as the hellions do.

Totally focused on all things flying mammalian, I used my transformative powers to turn myself into a bloodthirsty bat. My nose shriveled down into a pug muzzle. My teeth sharpened into fangs. My ribs crunched out to form the articulated skeletal scaffolding for a pair of thin-skinned wings.

When all I could see was a glowing green radar screen, I squealed, fluttered out my webbed wings, and flew back up that mineshaft with the rest of the repulsively scuzzy flock.

Honestly? The whole bat thing was pretty disgusting. I don't know how Bruce Wayne deals with it.

Chapter 1

TIME FOR ALIEN Hunter Tip Number 46: Always have an exit strategy, preferably one that doesn't involve transforming yourself into a flying rodent with rusty-gutter breath from guzzling way too much iron-rich hemoglobin.

Coming out of the bat transformation, I felt wiped. My mind was totally blown. My retinas had burnt-in blip spots from doing time as radar screens.

But at least I was me again.

I had lost the black cloak and the bat wings. I was back in a T-shirt, blue jeans, and sneakers, catching my breath outside a cave entrance. I had come to this abandoned West Virginia coal mine after picking up a hot tip on Number 2's possible location. The intel had been solid. I had definitely found the despicable Deuce's hidey-hole. My next problem: What to do about him, not to mention his massive army? How could I stop these extraterrestrial terrorists from destroying every city, town, and village on their hit list?

Still groggy, I retrieved my backpack, which I'd hidden deep inside a rock niche outside the cave. I fished out the super-thin, higher-than-high-tech alien laptop that has been my mission bible since day one and flipped open the lid. I needed to consult The List of Alien Outlaws on Terra Firma, which is what those of us from other parts of the galaxy call Earth.

I also needed to recharge my batteries. For me to rearrange molecules to create whatever my imagination cooks up, I need to be super calm and concentrate like crazy. If I'm tired or cranky, forget about it. At that moment I don't think I could've materialized a Double Whopper with cheese, even though I sort of wished I could. Bats burn up a ton of calories, what with the wing flapping and all that internalized radar action. I was famished.

The List thrummed to life in my lap. Much to my surprise, Balloon Boy—the bloated bullfrog I had called 30-something—was actually Number 29. Guess the freakazoid had shot up a slot or two after I erased a couple of his superiors in alien hunts past.

However, slot 29 was as high as Floating Froggy would ever hop. The constantly self-updating List was already flashing TERMINATED next to his name and number.

I swiped my fingers through the air and The List, fully annotated with illustrations, scrolled up the screen to exactly what I needed to see.

The entry for Number 2.

For some bizarre-o reason, the computer continued to pretty much draw a blank on the guy. Yes, there was a list of his known physical appearances (apparently he was a world-class shape-shifter, just like me), but under Planet of Origin, all I saw was CLASSIFIED. Same thing with Evil Deeds Done. CLASSIFIED. Powers? CLASSIFIED.

Classified? Hello, computer—you work for *me*, remember?

I gave the computer a good whack on the side. Yes, it's an extremely low-tech solution, but one that sometimes works, even with the galaxy's coolest, most artificially intelligent gizmos.

Not this time. The images on the screen refused to budge. Number 2's background would remain a mystery. A CLASSIFIED mystery.

I realized I needed to forget about where Number 2 came from and what he had already done, and focus instead on where he said he was going (all over the planet) and what he planned on doing once he and his army got there (wiping out human civilization and enslaving millions, not to mention making my life totally miserable).

Still glued to the uncooperative computer screen, I felt a not-so-gentle tap on my shoulder.

Startled, I whipped around.

Suddenly I was face-to-face-to-face-to-face with a four-sided killing machine.

Chapter 2

"WELL, WELL, WELL, well," the thing said, chortling in quadraphonic surround sound.

Then all of the blockhead's faces grinned.

"How frightfully convenient! Number 2 commissions us to go find Daniel X and, lo and behold, I find you hiding right outside our super-secret meeting place."

I, of course, immediately recognized the cubic jerkonium. It was hard not to. The creature was a four-sided warrior from the planet Varladra, complete with two pairs of brutal arms clutching four extremely lethal weapons: a scimitar the size of a scythe, a quarto-headed battle-ax, a classic nine-ring Chinese broadsword, and—just in case he got tired of flailing his limbs and swinging steel—what looked like a semi-automatic, rapid-repeating disintegrator gun.

Having just eyeballed The List, I knew exactly who (make that *what*) I was dealing with: Number 33 in my top forty countdown.

"Prepare to die, traitor!" sneered the clanking cube.

"No thanks," I said. "By the way, is Rubik your uncle or your aunt?"

He growled and swung his ax, aiming for my head like my neck was the tee and my skull the ball.

I ducked into a crouch. He whiffed.

"*Stee-rike* one," I said.

Number 33 rotated ninety degrees to the left, jangling the belt of human and alien skulls he wore wrapped around his squarish waist. Swishing blades twirled and whirled on all sides of his chest. It was like fighting a berserk food processor. The boxy behemoth only had two stubby legs, but both were mounted on rolling swivels. Number 33 was definitely turning out to be hell on wheels.

He tried a downward log-splitting lumberjack chop with the battle-ax—the one with *four* razor-sharp blades.

I was supposed to be the log.

I rolled right. Again, he whiffed.

"*Stee-rike* two!"

He yanked his ax head out of the dirt with one arm and used two of the others to swing his Chinese broadsword and slash at me with the scimitar.

I dodged, then ducked.

Two swings. Two misses.

"*Stee*-rikes three and four!"

I guess the official rules of baseball are different on Varladra, because he kept taking swings. I kept countering: juking and sidestepping, bobbing and weaving.

I needed to figure out this creep's weakness, and fast.

Fighting this four-sided death machine was a lot like taking on four Attila the Huns at the same time.

I darted left to avoid a flying triple parry and follow-up double thrust.

Man, the guy's aim was definitely off. Maybe he needed four pairs of glasses for his four pairs of eyes. Maybe he was still blind as a bat.

I checked out his flat noses, swarthy complexion, and wispy Fu Manchu beards.

Wait a second.

Number 33 *was* Attila the Hun, one of the most fearsome Eurasian nomads to ever invade Rome and earn the name "Barbarian." Or he *had* been Attila, back in the early to mid fifth century. All he needed was a fur-lined helmet and a woolly vest. This killing machine had been on Earth for sixteen centuries and he'd never been beaten. Talk about your heavyweight champion of the world.

"Stand still, boy!" Attila growled at me. "Do not prolong the inevitable."

"What's the matter, *hon*?" I said, still flitting around like a hummingbird stoked on liquid sugar. I couldn't resist the pun. "Have a rough day pillaging and plundering?"

Cube-head sneered at me. I could see chunks of meat snagged between his rotting teeth.

"Prepare to die, weakling!"

"Sorry. No way am I letting you and your mongrel horde of mutant misfits destroy human civilization."

"Foolish boy! This planet belongs to whoever or whatever is strong enough to take it!"

"Or defend it!"

Attila swiped a couple of hands roughly across a few of his slobbering mouths.

"Enough," he said. "It is suppertime, and I am most hungry. Therefore, submit to me and die!"

Up came the disintegrator gun.

Good thing I finally figured out how to beat this guy.

In a flash, I turned myself into a bubbling hot pot of yak stew.

Yum.

Chapter 3

ATTILA THE GORILLA must've been seriously starving.

He immediately grabbed the pot of meaty yak gruel and tossed it into his mouth. That is, he grabbed *me* and threw me down his gullet in a single gulp.

Over the teeth, over the gums, look out stomach, here I come.

I slid into his esophagus and cannonballed down the quivering chute into his gut.

They say the way to an alien's heart is through his stomach, and that was my plan: get digested, clog his arteries, and attack his heart!

Of course, when they say that thing about the stomach and heart, they leave out the bit about how, in between, you have to spend a little quality time down in the bowels. Remember to hold your nose when we get there.

I splashed into a pool of burbling acid and bobbed around with milky chunks of half-digested french fries, the gooey remains of a Snickers bar, and what might've once been creamed corn. Attila's stomach looked exactly like that Rubbermaid barrel full of pig slop the high school cafeteria guy scrapes all the dirty dishes into.

I sloshed forward, trying to avoid a McNugget oil slick. I needed to act like a bran muffin and move things along his digestive tract—fast. So I swam downstream as quickly as yak stew can.

Now, in order for me to get into Number 33's bloodstream and give him some serious heartburn, I needed to be a nutrient by the time I reached his small intestine. If not, my whole plan (and me with it) would go straight down the toilet. Literally.

As I was funneled into the stomach's exit ramp, I transformed myself into a glob of yak fat and, after a quick bile bath, moved into the small intestine. I thought I might hurl. The narrow, undulating tube smelled worse than any sewer I've ever had the pleasure of crawling through.

Fortunately, I didn't have to deal with the bowel stench for long, because I was instantly sucked through the intestinal lining. Just like that, I was cruising through Number 33's circulatory system.

If I could make it into his arteries—which had to be unbelievably clogged with sixteen hundred years' worth of Mongolian barbecue, mutton dumplings, and fried goat cheese—maybe I could completely block a blood vessel and shut his heart down.

Upstream, I could hear his heart muscle pounding out a four-four beat like a quartet of thundering kettledrums.

Because he had four hearts!

If I blocked the blood flow to one, the other three might be able to compensate.

Okay. I needed a plan B, as in "Blow up" or "ka-Boom."

The vein I was log-flume riding through splashed me down inside one of Attila's throbbing hearts. As I shot through one of its valves, I made myself morph again.

I hung on to the flapping valve with both hands as I began to change back into me—the full-sized, five-foot-ten Daniel X. I started to expand inside his cramped heart chamber like one of those Grow Your Own Girlfriend sponge toys that's guaranteed to grow 600 percent when you soak it in a bowl of water overnight.

Only I grew much bigger and much faster. Call it a teenage growth spurt.

I shattered his heart and burst through that alien's ribcage like the alien in *Alien*.

Blood spurting all around me (picture ketchup squeeze bottles gone wild), I watched Number 33—gasping and gurgling and clutching what was left of his chest—topple to the ground.

Attila the Hun was now Attila the Done.

Meanwhile, I was a little wet, somewhat sticky, and totally grossed out.

But I would live to fight another day. And another alien.

Number 2.

Clearly the most formidable and fearsome foe I have ever faced.

For more information on Daniel X go to
www.daniel-x.co.uk

We support

National
Literacy
Trust

I'm proud to be working with the National Literacy Trust, a great charity that wants to inspire a love of reading.

If you loved this book, don't keep it to yourself. Recommend it to a friend or family member who might enjoy it too. Sharing reading together can be more rewarding than just doing it alone, and is a great way to help other people to read.

Reading is a great way to let your imagination run riot – picking up a book gives you the chance to escape to a whole new world and make of it what you wish. If you're not sure what else to read, start with the things you love. Whether that's bikes, spies, animals, bugs, football, aliens or anything else besides. There'll always be something out there for you.

Could you inspire others to get reading? If so, then you might make a great Reading Champion. Reading Champions is a reading scheme run by the National Literacy Trust. Ask your school to sign up today by visiting www.readingchampions.org.uk.

Happy Reading!

James Patterson